HERE SIT I, WILLOW THOUGHT, WITH MY "DATE."

From her spot on the couch next to Willow, Cordelia frowned. "I mean, with Xander it's always 'Buffy did this' or 'Willow said that.' Buffy, Buffy, Willow, Willow. It's like I don't even exist."

Willow nodded, inwardly marveling that she could be so totally in sync with what Cordelia was thinking. Surely this would put a bad spin on the universe. "He's so busy looking around at everything he doesn't have that he doesn't even realize what he *does* have."

A part of Willow was rather horrified that she was in a semi-bonding conversation with, of all people, Cordelia.

"Yeah," Willow agreed. "Him and Xander. *Guys.*"

Cordy sat back in a huff. "Who do they think they are?"

"A couple of *guys,*" Willow answered sagely. They nodded in agreement—

And something huge and hairy fell from the ceiling and crashed onto their table.

Buffy the Vampire Slayer™

Buffy the Vampire Slayer (movie tie-in)
The Harvest
Halloween Rain
Coyote Moon
Night of the Living Rerun
The Angel Chronicles, Vol. 1
Blooded
The Angel Chronicles, Vol. 2
The Xander Years, Vol. 1
Visitors
Unnatural Selection
The Angel Chronicles, Vol. 3
The Power of Persuasion
The Willow Files, Vol. 1

Available from ARCHWAY Paperbacks and Pocket Pulse

Buffy the Vampire Slayer adult books

Child of the Hunt
Return to Chaos
The Gatekeeper Trilogy
   Book 1: Out of the Madhouse
   Book 2: Ghost Roads
   Book 3: Sons of Entropy
Obsidian Fate
Immortal
Sins of the Father

The Watcher's Guide: The Official Companion to the Hit Show
The Postcards
The Essential Angel
The Sunnydale High Yearbook
Pop Quiz: Buffy the Vampire Slayer

Available from POCKET BOOKS

BUFFY
THE VAMPIRE
SLAYER™

THE WILLOW FILES
Vol. 1

A novelization by Yvonne Navarro
Based on the hit TV series created by Joss Whedon
Based on the teleplays "I, Robot...You, Jane"
by Ashley Gable & Thomas A. Swyden,
"Phases" by Rob DesHotel & Dean Batali,
and "Dead Man's Party" by Marti Noxon

POCKET PULSE
New York   London   Toronto   Sydney   Singapore

This book is a work of fiction. Names, characters, places and incidents are products of the author's imagination or are used fictitiously. Any resemblance to actual events or locales or persons, living or dead, is entirely coincidental.

An *Original* Publication of POCKET BOOKS

 POCKET PULSE, published by
Pocket Books, a division of Simon & Schuster Inc.
1230 Avenue of the Americas, New York, NY 10020

™ and copyright © 1999 by Twentieth Century Fox Film Corporation. All rights reserved.

ISBN: 0-671-03918-0

First Pocket Pulse printing December 1999

10 9 8 7 6 5 4 3 2 1

POCKET PULSE and colophon are registered trademarks of Simon & Schuster Inc.

Printed in the U.S.A.

This one's for my Mom,
who showed me years ago
how much fun the dark side could
be by telling me about
Salem's Lot.

Acknowledgements

Thanks to Christopher Golden and Nancy Holder for steering me toward the written part of *Buffy,* and to Lisa Clancy, who's so much fun to work with. As always, the efforts of my agent, Howard Morhaim, are immensely appreciated.

Thanks, too, to Podmates Debbie Herbert and Pat Dillman at R&W, as well as dozens of other wonderful people there who gave me support and wished me luck.

And thanks most of all to my Dad, for giving the dream a place to live while it's coming true.

THE FILES

DAILY JOURNAL ENTRY:

Sometimes it so isn't easy to remember that I'm supposed to be *me*.

Things have always been...weird in Sunnydale, and at least now that Buffy's here I can find some logic behind the weirdness. Well, if you can call it logic to discover that your town hides the entrance to Hell and is a haven for vampires and...all kinds of other monsters. Every now and then I wake up wondering if I've gone crazy and I just don't know it—maybe this is just an insane story playing inside my head. You know, the first time I saw Buffy at the water fountain with Cordelia, I kind of thought she was just another one of Cordy's followers. Instead, she turns out to be The Slayer, like the one person in the world who can save Sunnydale and everyone in it from total doom. Which makes her far cooler than Cordelia or any homecoming queen will ever be. And the best part? It's *me*, Willow Rosenberg—the school's biggest bookworm and the invisible girl next door—who's somehow ended up with a superhero for a best friend!

I mean, who would've guessed that Rupert Giles would turn out to be anything more than a cool librarian—how rare is *that* to begin with? There he is, this old guy with a British accent . . . and a bizarre collection of antique books about strange monsters. I still thought he was just the librarian—like I thought Buffy was just the new girl from Los Angeles.

Oh . . . and I thought we'd all live forever.

I don't tell anyone, but I spend a lot of time thinking about Jesse and . . . well . . . wondering how afraid he was when the vampires took him underground. I guess I'm lucky I didn't have to, you know, see him after he was *changed*. I know Buffy tried her best to save him, even though it was her first day at school and everything. I could tell she was as surprised to find out about Sunnydale as Xander and I were. Poor Xander—I get to remember Jesse as the same goofy guy he always was. Thank goodness I didn't run into him at the Bronze the night of the Harvest! Still, while it's a . . . challenge to get used to some of the stuff, I think I've handled the truth about the Hellmouth well—and it beats the daily dull-o-rama that was my life before Buffy.

But . . . well, sometimes that's the problem.

Don't get me wrong. I mean, Buffy is my best girlfriend and Xander is my best boyfriend. Well, not boyfriend *boyfriend*—we're not dating or anything. I don't think Xander would even notice me unless I looked like the Barbie doll he stole from me when I was five. But in Life Before Buffy...at least I felt I had a *chance* with Xander. You know, that maybe someday he'd stop fooling around long enough to realize that, *duh*, I'm actually an air-breathing human *girl* instead of Pal Willow? Now...shoot. All he thinks, breathes and speaks: *Buffy*. I'm just the one he and everyone else can run to...when they have to write an English paper or cram for a biology test.

But that's okay—I mean, I don't mind it. I guess. That's a part of who I am, too. Willow Rosenberg, red-haired *A-1* student, okay sense of humor (I try, anyway). The Net Girl, okay, kind of a bookworm but with a taste for cool clothes from the sixties. Caffeine-free. That's not so bad, is it? I mean, it's just part of life when the boy you like has a thing for your best friend. Happens all the time on television...why should it be any different for me?

Because this is Sunnydale, darn it—*everything* is different here. Buffy has her own calling—The Slayer—and Xander is just...Xander. Mr. Perpetually Goofy with a comeback for nearly every sentence on the face of the earth—he can even hold his own with Cordelia Chase. Well, most of the time. Speaking of which, Cordelia has her own following—those hang-on-her-every-word Cordettes that trail after her like puppies slobbering after Biscuit Girl. I should have something, too, don't you think? I mean, besides good grades and a computer and lots of books. Which I love and would never give up for anything in the whole world.

See, this is high school, doggone it. All the other girls have boyfriends . . . or at least guys like Xander tagging after them and who would be boyfriendly if they could just find the right how-to manual. Some of them have been going steady with the same person since seventh or eighth grade—or earlier! And here's me, still so stuck on Xander after all these years. I mean, why can't I get him to realize that I wasn't really *that* angry at him for taking that stupid doll when we were in kindergarten?

You know what would be so awesome? If I found a boyfriend of my own—a "significant other" who *wasn't* Xander Harris. Not that I'd be trying to make Xander jealous . . . but it sure would show him a thing or two, wouldn't it?

Maybe the boyfriend problem is just that: a *problem* that needs to be solved. And darn it—I'm good with schoolwork and math and, well, problem *solving*. This whole one-on-one, boy-meets-girl thing—it's like . . . an equation. Yeah, but just a little more complicated. If I put a little effort into it, I could figure it out just fine. Sure I could—it's not really so hard. Is it?

One plus one equals two.
Girl meets boy.
Boy meets girl.
And . . . *voilà*.
Problem solved.

/PRESS ENTER TO SAVE FILE/

FILE:
I Robot, You Jane

PROLOGUE

ITALY: THE MIDDLE AGES

The walls were made of stone and rough-hewn wooden planks, unadorned and damp, heavy with the smell of the night and the men in the room. The scattered candles and glow of the flames in the fireplace did little to break the darkness. When a brown-haired young man stepped forward and took his place in front of his three companions, all four raised their faces reverently toward the creature seated on the oversized wooden chair a few feet away. Hushed and smiling, his face filled with youthful innocence, the first of the young men dropped slowly to his knees and clasped his hands, his gaze never wavering.

On the chair, Moloch the Corruptor smiled upon his worshiper and reached out. "Carlo, my dear one . . ." Moloch's enormous charred-black fingers were twisted and long, each ending in a claw that tapered to a knife-sharp point. As gently as a mother stroking her child, Moloch nodded his great, horned head as he rested his hand upon the young man's hair. At his touch, the boy's trusting smile widened to one of rapture.

"Do you love me?" Moloch asked. His eyes gleamed redly in the firelight, like rubies amid the creases of his leathery face. "I will give you *everything*. All I want is your love."

The young man's eyes were still alight with devotion as Moloch's grip tightened. Then the demon's wrist twisted, snapping his disciple's neck.

In a monastery a few miles away, a dozen monks gathered. Young and old, but the length of one's life mattered little in this most secret of rooms deep within the holy building. Here, it was belief that set them apart from the others of their order, and age gave only the knowledge of what must be done and the responsibility to see it through.

Brother Thelonius, his own face lined with years and worry beneath the fringe of his thinning hair, cradled a heavy book with an ornate cover in his arms as he moved to the center of the room. "It is Moloch," he told the rest of his brethren. "The Corruptor. He walks again. More and more of our people have fallen under his mesmerizing power."

Faces knotted in fear, the others stared at him. Still, he saw determination in their expressions.

"We must form the circle," Brother Thelonius instructed. "Now—there is still time to bind him!"

The monks obeyed without question, moving instinctively until Thelonius became the center of their group, his thin but strong form like the spoke of a mystical wheel. His fingers stroked the hideous engraving on the book's cover once, then he opened it. The light of the room's lamps and fire shone golden on the utterly blank pages, and the assembled monks began to chant in Latin.

On the hearth, the fire leapt and danced as a sudden

chilly wind swept along the chamber floor. In the room's far corners, the candles barely held their small flames as the monks' chanting swelled and filled the air.

"By the power of the Circle of Kayless, I command you, demon—*come!*" Brother Thelonius paused for a beat, then smiled fiercely as he realized victory would, indeed, be theirs.

"*I command you,*" he bellowed. "*COME!*"

Smiling with contentment, Moloch opened his fingers and let his young victim's body drop to the stone floor. His fire-filled eyes sought those of the next young man's, but before Moloch could beckon him forward, a sound filled the room, heating up the dank drafts surrounding him.

"No," he hissed, and started to rise as his remaining three worshipers looked around in confusion. "*No!*" He heard the words then, faint at first but finally clear enough to be understood—

"*I command you . . . COME!*"

—and Moloch the Corruptor began to scream and claw at the air around him. As his followers cowered in mortal terror, his massive and once-terrifying figure dissolved into bits of golden light and simply . . .

Swirled away.

Despite the wind screaming through the room, Brother Thelonius felt the book vibrate within his grasp. When he looked down, he saw heavy, dark writing splash across the once-pristine pages, true evidence of their triumph. As the monks' chanting ended, he closed the heavy cover of the book with a final *thud*.

Within the hour, Thelonius and the others had built a crate to hold the volume, then had chosen a hiding place for it within the darkest, deepest vault of the monastery.

As he sealed the crate and his brethren looked on, his weathered face seemed even more lined, marked by weariness and ongoing fear.

"Pray," he told them all solemnly, "that this accursed book shall never again be read, lest the demon Moloch be loosed upon the world."

And with the last of his strength, Brother Thelonius lifted in place the weighty top of the crate and firmly sealed it.

CHAPTER 1

"Oh," Buffy said. "Great. A book."

Willow Rosenberg looked over from her position in front of one of the scanners and smiled when she saw the disappointed expression on her friend's face. Buffy Summers pulled an oversized, ancient-looking book from the crate she'd just pried open and idly traced the carving on its leather cover. Jenny Calendar, the new computer science teacher, had set up several computers and scanners throughout the library. They were a jarring contrast to what Willow had always felt was the old-world charm of the book-filled room.

"I haven't gone through the new arrivals," Rupert Giles told Buffy. He gestured toward where Willow stood. "Put it in that pile—"

"Here, I've got it." Dave, a shy, bookish kid with thick blond hair, took the book from Buffy and headed back to his terminal. Next to him, a boy named Fritz worked diligently. Fritz was big and sturdily-built with short hair, the opposite of Dave. But like Willow, both were whizzes in the computer world.

"Thanks, Dave." Buffy grinned. "The Willow pile."

"After I've examined it," Giles said absently, "you can, uh . . . skim it in."

"Scan it, Rupert. *Scan* it."

The door to the library closed behind Ms. Calendar as she strode in and Willow had to hide her smile at the flustered set to Giles's jaw. If Fritz and Dave were different, then Ms. Calendar and Giles had to be polar opposites, literally repelling each other. Where Giles was like the library, old-world and rather charming despite the tweed-saturation level, Ms. Calendar was young and hip. She might have been thirty, but her hair was dark and cut short, and the way she dressed was a slightly more modest version of the rest of the girls in school.

"Of course," Giles said. His tone was filled with stiff British courtesy, but Willow thought she could hear a touch of venom around the edges.

Ms. Calendar, however, was not put off. "I know our ways are strange to you," she said as she regarded the librarian with patient amusement, "but soon you will join us in the twentieth century . . . with several years to spare!"

"Ms. Calendar," Giles said archly, "I happen to believe that one can function in modern society with*out* being a slave to the idiot box."

Ms. Calendar did an admirable job of holding her expression, although Willow could tell she really wanted to chuckle. "That's TV—the idiot box is the TV. This is a *good* box."

"Well," Giles said, undaunted. "I still prefer a good book."

"The printed page is obsolete," Fritz put in. His stance at his terminal was so relaxed that he might have been a part of the machine. "Information isn't bound up anymore, it's an entity. The only reality is virtual. If you're not jacked in, you're not alive." With that, he nodded to himself and flicked the OFF switch on his computer. A moment later the door to the library closed behind him.

They all stared after him, then Ms. Calendar sighed. "Thank you, Fritz, for making us all sound like crazy people." She turned back to Giles. "Fritz comes on a little strong, but he has a point. You know, for the last two years there was more E-mail sent than regular mail? More digitalized information went over phone lines than conversation."

Giles folded his arms and his chin lifted. "That is a fact I regard with genuine horror."

"I'll bet it is," Ms. Calendar replied. She faced Willow and the others. "All right, guys. Let's wrap it up for the day."

Willow glanced at the stack of waiting books, then back at her terminal. She hated to leave stuff undone—it always came back to haunt you the next morning. "I've just got a few more to do," she told Ms. Calendar. "I'll hang around for a bit."

"Cool," the computer teacher said with a smile. "Thanks."

"Xander," Willow said before her friend could head out after the others, "you want to stay and help me?"

Xander Harris paused, but only for a moment. "Are you kidding?"

"Yes," Willow said gently. "It was a joke I made up."

Xander nodded in relief. "Willow, I love you, but bye."

"I'll see you tomorrow," Willow called.

But she might as well have been talking to the wall. "Buffy," Xander yelled, heading into the hall. "Wait up!"

Willow watched him go and pressed her lips together. *I will not pout,* she told herself. *It's not becoming to a redhead. To a smart redhead.* Resigned, she went back to work and from a few tables over, Giles spoke to Ms. Calendar.

"I have to stay and clean up," he said stiffly. "I'll be back in the Middle Ages."

Willow looked over to see Ms. Calendar, without so much as cracking a smile as she walked out, give her parting comment to Giles:

"Did you ever leave?"

The hours flew past, as they always did when she worked on computer projects. The Internet, E-mail, on-line research—they were all incredible time-burners. Sometimes Willow thought they sucked up chunks of life like the Sunnydale vampires sucked up blood. Despite her intention to stay only a little while, it was already late night, but at least the book in front of her, the leather-covered one that Buffy had uncrated just before everyone left, was the last one.

Willow opened it to the first page, grateful to find that even though it was weighty, the pages were thick and not numerous. After naming the file WILLOW/BOOK12, she carefully drew the scanner down the first page, keeping her eyes on the screen to make sure the image didn't blur or distort. While she couldn't understand the strange characters and foreign words, the information seemed to be transferring cleanly and rapidly.

Almost done, she thought in relief. *Then I can go home and get started on my other homework.*

Great.

Turned slightly to the right and with her gaze focused on the screen, Willow never noticed the pages of the book as she completed and turned each one, never saw the way the ancient words and symbols appeared to slip off the heavy parchment as the scanner passed over them. When the last of the book's content entered the screen, Willow saved the file without looking back at the book, then glanced around the empty library one last time.

On the computer, the screen suddenly went blank. After a beat, three words appeared, one letter at a time, across the center:

WHERE AM I?

Willow hit the OFF button automatically. Finished at last, she gathered up her books and headed out of the library.

CHAPTER 2

Walking the corridors of Sunnydale High School in the morning was like threading your way through Neiman Marcus at the height of a huge sale on Christmas Eve. Noise, people, kids laughing and fighting and generally horsing around. But Willow sailed smilingly through the horde like it was nothing more than a few people in an uncrowded Weatherly Park.

"Willow—Willow! Hey, wait up!"

Buffy's voice cut through the din just as she caught up with her friend. Hugging her books, Willow gave her a welcoming grin. "Buffy! I didn't even see you."

Buffy squinted at her. "Or hear me. What was up last night?" she asked as they started walking again. "I tried your line like a million times."

"Oh, I was . . ." Willow hesitated. "I was talking," she finally finished.

Buffy made a gesture with her hand for Willow to continue. "Talking to . . . ?"

Instead of answering, Willow only smiled.

"Okay, that's it," Buffy said. She tagged after Willow, clearly interested. "You have a secret and that is *not* allowed."

"Why not?"

"'Cause . . . there's a rule." Buffy's voice had taken on a petulant why-aren't-you-sharing-with-me? tone, and Willow just had to take pity.

"Well," she amended, "I sort of met someone."

"I knew it!" Buffy's face lit up with excitement. "This is *so* important! When did you meet?"

"Last week," Willow told her. "Right after we did the scanning project in the library."

Her friend's smile grew wider and she switched directions so she could look at Willow full in the face while they walked, like a skater doing a backward stroll. Her questions tumbled out. "Does he go here? What's his name? Have you kissed him? What's he like?"

Willow's mouth turned up with amusement. "No, Malcolm, no, and very nice," she said, answering everything in one shot.

Buffy flounced forward, but her excitement was still obvious. "You are a thing of evil for not telling me this right away!"

"Well," Willow admitted, "I wasn't sure there was anything to tell. But last night . . ." She hugged her books tighter. "Oh, we talked *all* night. It was amazing. He's so smart, Buffy, and he's romantic and we agree about *everything*."

"What's he look like?"

"I don't know," Willow answered cheerfully.

Buffy's mouth worked, but she seemed at a loss for

words as she followed Willow from the hallway into the computer lab.

"You've been seeing a guy and you don't know what he looks like." She blinked. "Okay—it's a puzzle. No, wait. I'm good at these—does it involve a midget and a block of ice?"

"I met him on-line," Willow said patiently.

"On line for what?"

Willow tilted her head and pointed at the computer she always worked on; realization settled over Buffy's face. "Oh, on-*line*. As in . . . right. Duh."

"Morning, kids." Willow and Buffy looked up as Ms. Calendar came into the lab. "Buffy, are you supposed to be somewhere?"

"I have a free," she replied.

"Cool. But this is lab time so let's make it a nice short visit, okay?"

Buffy nodded. "Oh, sure."

Willow quickly ran through her log-on procedure as Buffy perched on a chair next to her. The instant it made the connection, the computer screen flashed a message:

YOU HAVE MAIL!

"It's him!" Willow said excitedly as she opened the message.

I'M THINKING OF YOU.

"Oh, he's so sweet," Willow said, charmed.

Beside her, Buffy seemed less than impressed. "Yeah, he's a sweetie."

"What should I write back?" Willow asked. Her fingers were poised over the keyboard as she tried to think.

Buffy cleared her throat pointedly. "Willow, I think it's really great that you've got a cool pen pal, but ... don't you think you're kind of rushing into all this? You know what I mean?"

"I'm thinking of you, too," Willow blurted, talking as she typed. She almost hit the ENTER button, then gasped. "No—that's incredibly stupid!"

"Will," Buffy interrupted, "down girl. Let's focus here, okay? What do you really know about this guy?"

Willow sat back sullenly. "See, I *knew* you'd react like this."

"Like what?" Buffy demanded. "I just want to make sure you're careful, that's all."

"Buffy—"

"He could be different than you think."

"His name is Malcolm Black," Willow said with exaggerated care. "He's eighteen and he lives in Elmwood, which is about eighty miles from here. And he *likes* me."

"Short, tall, skinny, fat ... ?" Buffy looked at her expectantly.

"Why does everything have to be about looks?" Willow demanded, frustrated.

"Not everything," Buffy acknowledged. "But *some* stuff is. I mean, what if you guys get really, really intense and then you find out he ... has a hairy back?"

Willow's eyes widened as she considered this, then her jaw set. "Well, no. He doesn't talk like the kind of person who would have a hairy back. And anyway, that stuff doesn't matter when you really care about each other." She looked down at her hands. "Maybe I'm not his ideal either," she said softly.

"Hey," Buffy said. She put an understanding hand on Willow's arm. "I just want to make sure that he's good enough for you, that's all. I think it's great that you met someone."

"Hey." Both Willow and Buffy jumped as Fritz appeared on the other side of the cubicle divider without warning. "Are you *done?*"

Buffy stared at him, her hazel eyes widening. "What?"

"I'm trying to *work.*"

"Okay," Buffy said a little testily. *"Sorry."*

Fritz sank back onto his chair with enough noise to let the two girls know he was annoyed, then waited to see what, if anything, would happen. He still remembered being in here earlier, when it was only him and Dave working diligently at their computers in the quiet, with no one else to hear Dave's whispered words—

"Yes . . . I will. I promise."

—in response to the smooth but digitized voice coming from the computer's speakers. Only a moment ago the workspace on his own screen had wiped to a dizzying slide show as the school's student files were accessed. After hardly more than a few seconds, Buffy Summers's face had pixelized in front of him. Then, as quickly as it had appeared, it blinked away and was replaced by the words

WATCH HER.

Fritz had, he hoped, thrown a brick into the direction of the conversation Buffy had been trying to carry on with Willow.

But what would happen when he wasn't around?

Buffy glanced at Willow, then over to where Ms. Calendar sat at her own terminal, thankfully not noticing their exchange. "Boy, Fritz is even more charming than usual."

Willow frowned a little. "I don't know what his problem is lately."

Buffy stood. They both knew it was time for her to make tracks before Ms. Calendar realized she was still hanging around. "He needs to get out more," Buffy said. "Or ever." She looked at the computer, then at Willow, as though she wanted to say something more. Instead, Willow felt Buffy touch her on the arm again, then her friend strode away.

"Hey, Fritz," Ms. Calendar said from behind him. *It figures,* Fritz thought, that she'd show up now rather than three minutes earlier, when she could have been the one to derail the girls' talk about Malcolm. "I'm looking at the log," his teacher continued. "You and Dave are clocking a pretty scary amount of computer time."

She looked at him, obviously expecting an explanation. "New project," he said without turning around, and left it at that.

He could almost feel her curiosity. "Will I be excited?"

Fritz smiled coldly, thinking it was almost a shame Ms. Calendar couldn't see his face.

"You'll die."

Good-looking guy—probably a senior, with light brown hair and eyes. He sat on the stone stairs leading down and into the courtyard, staring in disbelief at the screen of his laptop.

"This isn't my report," he said as Willow passed. He wasn't really talking to her, so she paid him no mind, never registering his next, amazed words. " 'Nazi Germany was a model of well-ordered society?' I didn't write that!" He looked around angrily, as though he could pinpoint the guilty party. "Who's been in my files?"

Xander buzzed up behind her and slipped his hands over her eyes.

"Guess who?"

"Xander," she said without hesitation.

"Well, yeah. But keep guessing anyway."

"Uh . . . Xander," Willow said again.

He lowered his hands and skipped around to walk next to her. "I can't fool you. You see right through my petty char-ahde." He looked at her expectantly. "We going to the Bronze tonight?"

Willow shook her head, hoping he wouldn't be offended. "Not me. I think I'm gonna call it an early night."

Xander arched an eyebrow. "Oh . . . Malcolm, right? Yeah, I heard. But you're going to be missing out." He did a little jig as he walked, putting on his best comedic face. "I'm planning to be witty. I'm gonna make fun of all the people who won't talk to me."

"That's nice," Willow said absently. "Have a good time." Lost in her own thoughts and with a smile on her face, she ambled away.

"She certainly looks perky," Buffy said. Xander jumped and Buffy grinned at her success in sneaking up behind him.

Recovering, Xander glanced at Willow's retreating figure. "Yeah, color in the cheeks, a bounce in the step—I don't like it. It's not healthy." He sent a final, longing stare in Willow's direction, then turned back to Buffy. "So what about you? Bronze? No—you probably have to slay vampires or some lame endeavor like that." His face was full of exaggerated self-pity. "Everybody deserts me."

Buffy couldn't help laughing. "Check out the jealous man."

Xander frowned. "What're you talking about?"

"You're jealous!"

"Of what?"

"Willow's got a thang," Buffy teased, "and Xander's left hanging."

"That's meaningless drivel," Xander said firmly as he walked next to her. "I'm not interested in Willow like that."

"Yeah," Buffy said. "But you got used to being the belle of the ball."

"No, it's just . . ." He hesitated. "This Malcolm guy— what's his deal? Tell me you're not slightly wigged."

"Slightly," she agreed. "I mean, just not knowing what he's really like."

"Or who he really *is*," Xander pointed out as they stopped and faced each other. "I mean, sure he says he's a high-school student, but I could say I was a high-school student."

"You are."

"Okay," Xander said quickly. "But I could also say I was an elderly Dutch woman, get me? Who's to say I'm *not*? If I'm in the elderly Dutch chat room—"

"I get your point." Buffy frowned as things suddenly clicked into place. "I get your *point*. This guy could be *any*body. He could be weird, or crazy, or old or . . . he could be a circus freak—he's *probably* a circus freak!"

Xander's eyes were serious. "I mean, we read about that all the time. People meet on the net, they talk, they get together, have dinner, a show, horrible ax murder . . ."

Buffy's eyes widened as she contemplated this. "Willow, ax-murdered by a circus freak! Okay, okay—what do we do?"

They stared at each other, then Buffy gave herself a mental shake. "What *are* we doing?" She smacked her friend on the arm. "Xander, you get me started—we are totally overreacting!"

Xander gave her his crooked, one-of-a-kind grin. "Yeah," he said. "But isn't it fun?"

The computer lab was quiet and, other than Fritz, empty of people. He sat at his console and stared in wonder at the screen, watching complicated equations race by at what would have been an impossible pace for anyone else. He, however, had no problem deciphering them. *All* of them.

"I'm jacked in," he murmured happily. "I'm jacked in I'm jacked in I'm jacked in—"

Gaze fixed rigidly on the information scrolling furiously down the screen, he never realized he was carving the initial *M* into the skin of his forearm with an X-ACTO knife.

CHAPTER 3

Oh boy, Willow thought, more than a little panicked. *I can't* believe *how late I am.* She barreled up to her locker in the gym room, nearly colliding with Buffy as her friend shrugged into P.E. clothes.

"Whoa," Buffy said, between Willow's banging her books inside the metal locker. "You're the late girl."

"I overslept," Willow said shortly.

"Till fifth period?" Buffy stared at her, then looked away. "Talking to Malcolm last night?"

"Yeah." When Buffy didn't respond, Willow glanced at her. "What?"

"Nothing."

Willow searched frantically through her locker for the book she hoped to read while waiting for her turn on the gym floor. She hadn't studied last night and she desperately needed to do some catch-up before last period. "You're having an expression."

"I'm not." Buffy hesitated. "But . . . if I was, it would be saying this just isn't like you."

There it is. Willow snatched up the biology book and slammed her locker shut. "Not like me to have a boyfriend?"

Buffy's eyes widened momentarily. "He's . . . boy-friendly?"

"I don't understand why you don't want me to have this." Willow tried to keep the frustration out of her voice, but she wasn't succeeding. "I mean, boys don't chase me around all the time—I thought you'd be *happy* for me."

Buffy took a step toward her. "I just want you to be *sure.* To meet him face to face, in daylight, in a crowded place, with some friends. You know, before you become all obsessive."

Willow scowled. "Malcolm and I really care about each other. Big deal if I blow off a couple classes."

"I thought you said you overslept."

Caught, Willow didn't know what to say. Then she folded her arms protectively around her book. "Malcolm said you wouldn't understand."

She turned and walked off, but not before she heard her best friend's final comment.

"Malcolm was right."

Willow and Malcolm—Buffy worried over the thought all through P.E. When the boring class was finally over, she changed back into her regular clothes and headed over to the computer lab. Poking her head through the door, she spied Dave typing enthusiastically at one of the consoles.

"Hi, Dave," she said when she reached him.

There was no response, and Buffy glanced from him to the screen. The words there were moving too fast for her to read and Dave's fingers were a blur on the keyboard. She tried again. "Hi there, Dave."

Still no response. Obviously this boy needed human contact. "Anybody home?" she asked amiably and touched him on the shoulder.

He jumped and twisted on his chair. When he saw her, his expression seemed to tense up even more as he folded his hands in his lap, then he relaxed. "Oh. What do you want?"

"I wanted to ask you something," Buffy said. "If you have a minute."

Dave blinked, as if he were trying to gather his thoughts. "What is it?"

"Well," Buffy snagged the chair from the next console. She pulled it over, then perched on the edge. "You're a computer geek—" She cleared her throat and covered her blunder. "Genius. I sort of have a technical problem. If I wanted to find out about someone, if someone E-mailed me, could I trace the letter?"

Dave shrugged and pushed away the thick lock of hair that had fallen into his eyes. "Well," he told her, "you can pull up someone's profile based on their user name."

Buffy considered this. "But . . . they write the profile themselves, right? So they could say anything they want."

"Sure."

"Wow," she said. "I had knowledge."

Dave smiled and Buffy thought he might not have been half bad if he'd just get away from being hard-wired into machines all the time. She thought for a moment. "Well, is there a way to find out exactly where a letter—an E-letter— came from? I mean, the actual *location* of the computer?"

Dave looked thoughtful. "It's a challenge."

She felt obliged to explain. "'Cause you see, Willow's got this friend Malcolm," she said, "and to tell you the truth, I—"

"Leave Willow alone," Dave said. His voice was suddenly cold, his face white.

Buffy sat back. "What do you mean?"

"That's none of your business." Dave turned his back abruptly.

Buffy slowly stood and pushed the chair she'd borrowed back to its place. "Dave," she asked slowly, "are you . . . Malcolm?"

"Of course not."

"Dave, what's going on?"

"Nothing," he said harshly. He brought his fingers to the keyboard, but before he could start typing again Buffy snagged one of his hands in hers.

"Your hands," she said as she stared at his fingers. Every one of them was wrapped in Band-Aids.

"It's nothing," he said and yanked away from her. "I'm typing a lot."

"What's going on?" she demanded again.

"Look," he said. "I'll talk to you later, okay? I've got work to do."

He turned again to his console and left her standing there, clearly dismissed. She stared at his back for a second, then turned and stalked out of the lab.

"So do I," she muttered to herself.

She never noticed Fritz watching them surreptitiously from the other side of the divider, nor did she catch the murderous expression on his face.

Buffy found Giles in the library—big surprise there— and filled him in on what she knew so far. "I'm telling you, there's something going on," she finished. "It's not just Willow. Dave, Fritz—they're *all* wicked jumpy."

Giles didn't seem convinced. "Well, those boys aren't sparklingly normal as it is."

"Giles, *trust* me," Buffy said.

"I do." He paused. "But I really don't know how to advise you. Things involving the computer fill me with a childlike terror. Now if it were a nice ogre or some such, I'd be more in my element." At her sour glance, he shrugged. "Well, I suppose you could 'tail' Dave, see if he's up to something."

Buffy looked at Giles in amazement. "*Follow* Dave? What, in dark glasses and a trench coat? Please. I can work this out myself." She stopped for a second, thinking. "Willow's been acting weird since we scanned those books; Fritz has been acting weird since birth. I don't know—I've got all the pieces, but no puzzle. Or I've got puzzle pieces but some of them are missing. Or they're in the wrong place in the puzzle."

Her mouth turned down. "I hate metaphors. I'm gonna follow Dave."

She thought she'd feel ridiculous in the sunglasses and trench coat get-up, but it was actually kind of cool and mysterious, like a character in a cop novel or something. Following Dave wasn't nearly as difficult as she'd thought it would be; his car was old and sickly and he seemed to catch every red light in town. Even though she was on foot, Buffy kept up easily and when he parked in a spot at the side of a large, blocky building surrounded by a high fence, she slipped unnoticed into an alcove next to the driveway entrance.

Hanging on the gate was a sign that spelled out CRD in large letters. Beyond the fence a half dozen eerily silent workmen were using dollies and a forklift to haul boxes into the building. When Dave joined them, an expressionless man in a scientist-type coat greeted him, then they went inside. The only one left on the dock was an equally blank-faced security guard. Buffy waited awhile, but no one came out and she felt there were too many people around to actually follow Dave into the building.

With little else to go on, she finally headed back to the high school.

The security room inside CRD was small and gray-walled, like being in a dull, dim box. This bothered Fritz not at all.

Sitting at a computer console, his unblinking gaze was focused on the video image of Buffy Summers as she stood just out of sight at the main gate and peered toward the loading dock.

"She's too close," he said. "What do I do?"

The image of Buffy, dressed like a Bogart-style private eye, stayed in place for a few seconds, then it blinked away to blackness. After a beat, two words appeared.

KILL HER.

Fritz read the command and a slow, nasty smile spread across his mouth.

"Party."

CHAPTER 4

The library again, the place where everything in her life seemed to end up. Well, except for the cemetery.

"Whatever Dave is into," Buffy told Giles and Xander, "it's large."

Giles looked at her with interest. "What was the name of the place?"

"Said CRD. I couldn't get close enough to see what it was—"

"Calax Research and Development," Xander cut in. "Computer research lab, third biggest employer in Sunnydale until it closed last year." When he saw Buffy and Giles gawking at him, he managed to look righteously offended. "What, I can't have information sometimes?"

"It's just somewhat . . . unprecedented," Giles said, flustered.

"Well, my uncle used to work there," Xander admitted. "In a floor-sweeping capacity."

Buffy looked thoughtful. "But it closed."

Xander nodded. "Uh-huh."

"Looked pretty functional from where I stood." She crossed her arms. "I don't have a clue what they were doing, though."

"And what do they need Dave for?" Xander wondered.

"Something about computers, right?" she suggested. "I mean, he is off-the-charts smart."

Giles shoved his hands into his pockets. "We still don't know a terrible lot. Whatever's going on there could be on the up and up."

Xander shook his head. "If CRD reopened, it would have been on the news."

Buffy lifted her chin. "Besides, I can just tell something's wrong. My spider-sense is tingling."

"Your 'spider-sense'?" Giles asked, puzzled.

"Pop culture reference," Buffy said by way of explanation. "Sorry."

Giles looked from one to the other. "Yes, well, I think we're at a standstill. Short of breaking into the place, I don't see—"

"Breaking in," Buffy said brightly. "This, then, is the plan."

"I'm free tonight," Xander offered.

Buffy nodded. "Tonight it is."

"A moment, please, of quiet reflection," Giles scolded. "I did *not* suggest that you illegally enter the—" He looked over Buffy's shoulder and suddenly his tone changed. "—data into the file, so the book will be listed by title as well as author."

Buffy and Xander turned and found Ms. Calendar joining them. "Hi," she said.

"Hello," Giles said, standing ramrod straight.

The computer science teacher smiled at Giles. "I just

came by to check your new database, make sure your cross reference table isn't glitching. Because I'm guessing you haven't gone near it."

Giles looked pained. "I'm still sorting through the *chaos* you left behind."

Ms. Calendar smiled thinly, then glanced at Buffy and Xander. "You here again? You kids really dig the library, don't you?"

"We're literary," Buffy said spritely.

"To read makes our speaking English good," Xander added.

Buffy nearly groaned. She snagged Xander's arm and pulled him toward the door. "We'll be going now."

"Yes," Giles said. His voice held a sharp edge. "We'll continue our conversation another time."

Buffy gave him a cheerful smile. "I think we're done." Before Giles could comment further, she hauled Xander out into the hallway. " 'Our speaking English is good'?" she demanded.

Xander had the good grace to look ashamed. "I panicked, okay?"

All she could do was shake her head as they hurried out of the school.

Good, Willow thought. *I've got the place to myself for a change.* She glanced around one more time just to make sure, then smiled as she read the words on the computer screen in front of her.

I'VE NEVER FELT THIS WAY ABOUT ANYONE BEFORE, WILLOW.

Her smile widened—she couldn't help it. "I know what you mean," she said, echoing the words aloud as she typed the return message to Malcolm. "I feel like you know me better than anyone."

I DO.

Willow took a deep breath. "Do you think we should . . ." She hesitated, then went for it. ". . . meet?" She hit the ENTER button before she could change her mind.

I THINK WE SHOULD SOON.

She swallowed and let her fingers type out the truth. "I'm nervous."

I'M NOT. ISN'T THAT STRANGE?

"That's what Buffy doesn't understand," Willow told Malcolm in her reply. "How comfortable you can make me feel."

BUFFY JUST MAKES TROUBLE. THAT'S WHY SHE GOT
KICKED OUT OF HER OLD SCHOOL.

Willow froze, unsettled. "How did you know that?" she typed.

IT'S ON HER PERMANENT RECORD.

She sat there, trying to digest this. *Buffy's permanent record? But how would Malcolm know that unless he had access to the files? And why would he want to, anyway?*

Another message from Malcolm suddenly appeared.

YOU MUST HAVE MENTIONED IT.

Willow stared at the words. Finally she typed the only thing she could think of to say. "I guess."

LET'S NOT WORRY ABOUT HER ANYMORE.

She hesitated, then decided things were just a little too freaky right now to continue. "I have to sign off," she typed decisively. "I'll talk to you later."

DON'T!

But her mind was made up. "Bye." She sent it and turned off the screen before Malcolm could try to dissuade her, then left the lab with a troubled look on her face.

Jenny Calendar regarded Rupert Giles with an odd mixture of humor and annoyance. "You're a snob."

"I am no such thing," Giles said defensively.

"Oh, you are a *big* snob," she repeated. "You think knowledge should be kept in carefully guarded repositories where only a handful of white guys can get at it."

"Nonsense," Giles said angrily and she almost laughed. She knew she'd find a way to get to him. "I simply don't adhere to a knee jerk assumption that because something is new, it's *better*."

Ms. Calendar held back another chuckle. "This isn't a fad, Rupert. We are creating a new society here!"

Giles drew himself up and she wondered if she should change "snob" to "stuffed shirt." *Same thing, really.* Wisely, she decided to keep quiet. "A society in which human interaction is all but obsolete," he said in an acid-tinged voice. "In which people can be completely manipulated by technology. Thank you, I'll pass."

She arched an eyebrow as she leaned against the edge of a table. "Well, I think you'll be very happy here with your musty old books." To emphasize her point, Ms. Calendar picked up an ancient-looking book next to her. After glancing at the carved leather cover, she began leafing through the pages.

Irritation infused Giles's next words. "These 'musty old books' have a great deal more to say than any of your fabulous web pages."

Ms. Calendar shot him a look. "Hm. This one doesn't have a whole lot more to say." She turned the book to face Giles and indicated the blank pages. "What is it, like a diary?"

Giles peered at it. "How odd. I haven't looked through all the volumes yet. I didn't—" He broke off as he closed the book and saw the elaborate horned image cut into the book's cover.

"What is it?" Ms. Calendar asked.

Giles remained silent for a moment. "Uh, nothing," he finally told her. "A diary. Yes—I imagine that's what it is."

She looked again at the grotesque creature portrayed on the book's front. "Nice," she commented. "You collect heavy metal album covers, too?"

"Yes," Giles said absently.

Ms. Calendar's mouth dropped open. "You do?"

"Well," Giles continued, "it's been so nice talking to you—"

"We were fighting."

"—and we must do it again sometime. Bye now."

Before she could retort, he strode away, the strange, blank book held firmly in hand.

Ms. Calendar thoughtfully watched him go. Puzzling

behavior, but there were other things peculiar lately, too—like the signs she'd picked up on in her circle of acquaintances on the Internet this morning. Giles's background would lend well to a discussion about it, but his "adamantly against" attitude about computers had kept her from actually bringing up the subject. *Oh well;* now that his ugly book had taken all his attention, it would just have to wait until a more opportune time.

"But I *checked* the computer!" Buffy heard one of the school nurses tell a teacher as she walked past the two outside the building. "And there's *nothing* in his file about being allergic to penicillin!"

Before Buffy could think further about what she'd heard, someone touched her arm. Turning, she saw Dave waiting to talk to her. "Buffy."

He seemed even more nervous than usual about being around real humans, so she felt compelled to be forgiving about his earlier weird-out. "Dave, how're you doing?"

"Okay." Despite his words, he wouldn't meet her eyes. Instead, he looked over her shoulder, at the sky, at the ground. Anywhere but at her face. "I'm . . . sorry about yesterday. I haven't been sleeping much."

"Don't sweat it."

He scuffed at the ground with one shoe. "Uh, Willow was looking for you."

Buffy brightened. "Oh, good, I need to talk to her. Do you know where she is?"

He shoved his hands deeper into his pockets. "She said she would be in the girls' locker room."

"Great," Buffy said again. Since Dave was clearly not quick enough to continue interacting with a nonwired female, she decided to let him off the hook. "Thanks," she added and headed away.

And in taking pity on him, Buffy completely missed the petrified look he gave her as she walked away.

Fritz waited calmly just inside the showers, listening to the sound of Buffy's footsteps. Everything was ready; he need only turn on the water at the right time, then silently slip out of the locker room and let fate do what it would.

Party.

"Will?"

Buffy moved through the totally empty locker room until she came to the end of the row. No one was around, and certainly not Willow. She was about to leave when she heard one of the showers start up, the sound of the water echoing off the walls.

"Willow?" she called. "Will, you taking a shower?" She angled her head around the corner, but the tiled shower area was empty. "Guess not." She glanced behind her, but there was still no one there. "This," she muttered as she stepped into the rapidly spreading puddle of water to turn off the faucet, "is how droughts get started."

"Buffy—get out!"

She spun in surprise and saw Dave standing at the other end of the locker room. His expression was full of horror and regret, his gaze frozen toward the wall at the opposite corner of the room. When she jerked in that direction, Buffy saw why: a cord dangled from a gutted light fixture high on the wall, the bare-ended wires lying on the floor—

Only a fraction of an inch away from the creeping puddle of water in which she now stood.

Instinct made her bolt for the exit to the locker room and one leap took her to the edge of the shower stall. Buffy jumped the rest of the way just as the water touched the wires; she felt the surge of electricity slam through her right before she hit the wooden bench, then rolled to the floor. She stayed there for a moment, stunned, feeling her nerves and skin tingle and trying to fathom what had just happened.

When she finally raised her head, Buffy saw the soles of both her shoes were blackened and smoking.

The shades were drawn and it was dim and cool in the computer lab, deserted in the late afternoon. A good thing, because Dave had no thought for anyone else as he rushed through the door and began pacing in front of his computer console. Without sitting down—there was no need—he began arguing with it as he strode back and forth like a trapped animal.

"I can't do it! I'm not *gonna* do it!"

From the small speaker attached to the side of the screen, a calm, metallic voice replied. The tone was deep and impersonal, and went along with the words appearing on the screen.

BUT YOU PROMISED.

"Buffy isn't a threat to you," Dave argued in response. "It's not worth it!"

THE PROJECT IS ALMOST COMPLETE.

YOU WON'T HAVE TO DO IT AGAIN.

Dave scrubbed at his face with his hands. "I *can't.*"

I'VE SHOWN YOU A NEW WORLD, DAVE.
KNOWLEDGE, POWER . . . I CAN GIVE YOU EVERYTHING.

ALL I WANT IS YOUR LOVE.

"No," Dave said with finality. "This isn't right. *None* of it is!"

I'M SORRY. I'VE BEEN A TERRIBLE PERSON.

Confused, Dave stopped and peered at the computer screen. Had he won the argument? Was—

I'M A COWARD AND I CAN'T GO ON
LIVING LIKE THIS. FORGIVE ME,
MOM AND DAD.

He stumbled backward, still focused on the dreadful words across the computer screen. What the—?

AT LEAST NOW I'LL HAVE SOME
PEACE. REMEMBER ME.

Dave took another step back, then felt the presence of someone standing behind him. Right before he heard the computer's final words, he whirled and saw Fritz waiting for him in the shadows with an awful, deadly smile across his face.

LOVE, DAVE.

CHAPTER 5

For a change, the library felt like a sanctuary to Buffy, a place where she could go and feel safe. A place to recover.

"I'm gonna kill Dave," Xander said. He strode across the floor in front of Buffy, so upset he was practically waving his arms.

"He tried to *warn* me," Buffy pointed out. She felt bleary and slow, frazzled at the ends.

"Warn you that he set you up!" Xander turned to Giles. "Is she going to be okay?"

Giles studied Buffy. "She was only grounded for a moment." He paused, then directed his next statement to her. "Still, if you'd been anyone but the Slayer . . ."

"Tell me the truth," Buffy said earnestly. She looked from Giles to Xander. "How's my hair?"

"It's . . . great," Xander answered. "It's your best hair ever."

"Oh, yes," Giles agreed.

She looked at them suspiciously. Beneath her fingers, her do felt shaggy and fly-away. She had the feeling it was a stunning example of why stuff like Cling-Free had been invented. Well, there was nothing to be done about it right now. "I just . . . I don't understand what would make Dave do a thing like that."

Giles cleared his throat. "I think perhaps I do."

Xander stopped his nervous motion. "Care to share?"

Giles pressed his lips together, then lifted an oversized book from one of the tables. "Does this look familiar to either of you?"

Buffy squinted at it through bangs that seemed to have a life of their own. "Yeah, sure. It looks like a book."

Xander nodded. "I knew that one."

"Well," Giles told them, "this particular book was sent to me by an archaeologist friend who found it in an old monastery."

Xander hid a fake yawn. "Wow, that's really boring."

Giles glared at him. "There are certain books that are not meant to be read. Ever. They have things . . . *trapped* within them."

"Things . . ." Buffy echoed.

Giles looked at the floor. "Demons."

Buffy rolled her eyes. "Here we go."

Giles took a deep breath. "In the Dark Ages, demons' souls were sometimes trapped in certain volumes. The demon would remain in the book, harmless, unless the book was read aloud." He pointed to the carved image on the cover, what Buffy considered to be an extremely ugly image of something resembling a ram and a flat-nosed . . . well, creature.

"Unless I'm mistaken," Giles continued, "this is Moloch the Corruptor. A very deadly and seductive demon. He draws people to him with promises of love, power, knowledge. He preys on impressionable minds."

"Like Dave's," Xander said.

Giles nodded. "Dave, and who knows how many others."

Buffy leaned forward. "And Moloch is inside that book?"

In reply, Giles flipped it open, showing them its blank pages. "Not anymore."

Xander's jaw dropped. "You released Moloch?!"

"Way to go," Buffy groaned.

"I didn't read it," Giles said testily. "That dreadful Calendar woman found it and it was already blank."

Buffy ran her hands through her hair, still trying to ignore the Brillo pad feel of it. "So a powerful demon with horns is walking around Sunnydale? And nobody's noticed?"

"If he's so big and strong," Xander demanded, "why bother with Dave? Why didn't he just attack Buffy himself?"

Giles dropped the blank book on the table. "I don't know. And I don't know who could have read the book. It wasn't even in English."

"Where was it?" Buffy asked.

Giles gestured toward the table with the computer on it. "In a pile with the other books that were . . ." He paused and his eyes went suddenly wide. "Scanned."

The threesome stared at each other, then they all turned toward the computer, sitting silent and apparently harmless a few feet away.

"Willow scanned all the new books," Buffy said quietly.

"And that released the demon," Xander added.

"No," Buffy said thoughtfully. "He's not out here." She pointed at the computer. "He's *in* there."

Giles took a few steps toward the machine, then stopped at what he must have thought was a safe distance. "The scanner read the book," he said slowly. "And brought Moloch out . . . as information to be absorbed."

Buffy nodded. "He's gone binary on us."

Xander held up a hand. "Okay, for those of us in our studio audience who are me, you guys are saying that Moloch is in this computer?"

Buffy looked at him. "And in every computer connected to it by a modem."

"He's everywhere," Giles said, clearly appalled.

Dismay spread across Xander's face. "What do we do?"

Buffy looked at Giles. "Put him back in the book?"

Giles seemed more than slightly lost. "Willow scanned him into her file. This may be a futile gesture, but I suggest we delete it."

"Solid," Buffy said. She slid onto the chair in front of the computer, cracked her knuckles, and turned on the CPU.

"Don't get too close," Xander said nervously.

"Okay, so which file do you think it is?" Buffy wondered aloud. She regarded the icons on the program screen. "Willow," she decided. "That's probably it, right? I'll . . . just delete the whole thing."

Without waiting, she positioned the cursor over the Willow file icon and dragged it over to the TRASH. Then she nearly jumped out of her seat as the computer's program screen abruptly flashed to black, then re-formed into a digitized image of Moloch the Corruptor himself. The image turned and grew until it filled every inch of the monitor, and suddenly a voice—hateful and loud—roared from the computer's tinny speakers.

STAY AWAY FROM WILLOW! IT'S
NONE OF YOUR BUSINESS.

* * *

And without her touching it, the entire computer shut down.

For a long moment, none of them moved.

" 'Stay away.' " Buffy paused. "That's just what Dave said when I asked about Willow and . . ." She looked at Giles and Xander. "Malcolm."

Xander's face went rigid. "What are you thinking?"

Buffy looked down and her gaze traveled to her mangled sneakers. "So that's what Malcolm looks like," she said quietly. "I'm wishing that Willow's new boyfriend was just an ax-murdering circus freak."

Ten minutes later, and they still hadn't figured out any better way to deal.

"Okay," Buffy finally said in disgust. "So much for 'delete file.' "

Giles's expression had grown darker by the minute. "This is *very* bad."

Xander still seemed only slightly convinced there was a true problem. "Are we overreacting?" he asked. "This guy's in a computer. What can he do?"

Buffy shot him an I-don't-believe-you-don't-get-it look. "You mean besides convince a perfectly nice kid to try and kill me?" She shrugged in fake carelessness. "I don't know—mess up all the medical equipment in the world?"

"Randomize traffic signals," Giles offered.

"Access launch codes for our nuclear missiles," Buffy suggested.

"Destroy the world's economy," added Giles.

Buffy looked at him. "I think I pretty much capped it with the nuclear missile thing."

Giles had to nod. "All right, yours was best."

Xander threw up his hands. "Okay, he's a threat. I'm on board with that now. But what do we do?"

Buffy tapped her fingers against the computer tabletop. "The first thing we do is find Willow," she decided. "She's probably talking to him right now. God, that creeps me out."

Xander scowled. "What does he want with Willow?"

The three of them looked at one another, but if Giles knew the answer, he wasn't inclined to share. "Let's never find out," Buffy finally said. "Okay, I'm gonna check the computer lab." She headed toward the door with a final instruction to Xander. "And you guys, call her home."

With that, she was out of the library and hurrying down the hall, much more frightened for her friend than she would have ever cared to admit.

The computer lab was a spacious, bright room, and Buffy was used to seeing it well-lit and seldom with fewer than two or three people in it. The dark room stretching in front of her now slowed her steps and made her cautious, but nothing was going to stop her from hunting for her best friend.

But the cubicle where Willow usually worked, about midway into the room, was empty—as was every other one. Before Buffy could ponder this, however, there was the electrical hum of equipment, then all the monitors flickered to life at once. Then they just . . . *sat* there, as if they were staring at her and waiting for something. Or some*one*.

"Willow?"

Suddenly the notion of going on to the door at the far end, past the line of silently watching computers, was too creepy. Turning, she checked behind her, as though she were inching away from a dog that was about to bite. She took a couple of steps, then another one, and another one—

Something bumped into her.

Buffy whirled, ready to fight. But instead of striking,

one tight fist came up to her mouth and she bit her knuckle in distress. Dave hung from a rope fixed to the ceiling, his corpse rocking from side to side, the rope creaking softly in the stillness.

"Dave . . ." Hesitantly Buffy reached out and stopped the sway of the body so she could read the note taped to his chest.

She didn't believe a word of it.

Buffy got back to the library in time to see Xander hang up the telephone. "No answer," he told Giles.

"Damn," the librarian said.

"Phone wasn't busy either, so she's not on-line." Then Xander realized Buffy was there. "She's not home."

Giles looked at her and frowned at her clouded expression. "What did you find?"

Xander's face suddenly drained of color. "Willow isn't—"

"Dave," Buffy said shortly. "He's dead."

"My God," Giles breathed.

Xander sat abruptly. "This is really *real*, huh?"

Giles stepped forward. "How—?"

"Well, it *looked* like suicide." Buffy folded her arms.

"With a little help from my friends?" Xander added sarcastically.

Buffy nodded. "I'd guess Fritz. Or one of the zomboids from CRD."

Giles was looking more upset by the second. "Horrible."

Buffy gestured at Xander. "Okay, you and I are going to go to Willow's house," she said before turning to Giles. "Giles, you need to come up with a way to get Moloch out of the net."

But Giles looked utterly bewildered. "I have records

of the ceremonies but that's for a creature of flesh. This could be something completely different—"

"Then get Ms. Calendar," Buffy said. "Maybe she can help you."

Giles's mouth worked but for a moment nothing came out. "Even if she could," he finally managed, "how am I going to convince her there's a demon on the Internet?"

"Okay, fine," Buffy said a little too flippantly. "Then you can stay here and come up with a better plan." She grabbed Xander's arm and hauled him toward the door. "Come on."

Giles watched them go, worry etched into his features.

It'd been a long day, and the last of that conversation with Malcolm was weighing heavily on Willow's thoughts. She'd stayed away from Buffy and Xander, intentionally avoiding the library even though she preferred to study there above anywhere else. Now she was glad to be home and away from school and friends who seemed to have endless questions about Malcolm—the same questions she was now afraid she couldn't answer.

She let herself in and carefully shut the door behind her. "Mom?" she called. "Dad?"

No one home, and maybe that was just as well, too. Willow climbed the stairs to her room, knowing she needed time to think things through and decide what, if anything, to do. She dropped her book bag on the bed and started to go through it, then jumped when her computer blipped and suddenly announced YOU HAVE MAIL!

Was it Malcolm? There was only one way to find out and a few keystrokes gave her the answer.

NO MORE WAITING. I NEED YOU TO SEE ME.

Malcolm's words blinked at her on the screen, vaguely threatening. Willow stared at them, unsure of what to do. Then, in one decisive move, she turned off the computer monitor and went back to emptying her book bag.

YOU HAVE MAIL!

She spun with a gasp and saw the monitor was on again—how had *that* happened? Freaked, she moved hesitantly toward the computer. What would he say now? How—

The doorbell rang.

Saved by the bell, Willow thought. Thank God for clichés. She glanced at the computer one more time, then scurried down the steps to see who was there. She already had a good idea, and when she pulled open the door, it was with a smile on her face. "Dad, did you forget your keys again?"

But there was no one there. Puzzled, Willow poked her head outside and glanced around—nothing. *A kid,* she thought, *playing a prank or something.* She turned to go inside, intent on drawing the door shut.

Something moved behind her, then a hand holding a chloroform-soaked rag clamped roughly over her mouth. She struggled but it was no use. Her attacker was big, the arm across her collarbone brawny and strong. She clawed at his hand, then sucked air involuntarily through the medicinal stink of the rag. Her consciousness began to fade immediately. The guy kidnapping her said something and in her mind, out of it or not, she recognized the voice as Fritz's.

NO MORE WAITING.

Willow slumped into oblivion as Fritz dragged her away.

CHAPTER 6

"*A spokesman for the Archbishop denied the error, blaming computer error for the apparent financial discrepancy. In Washington today, the FBI reported that all of its serial killer profiles had been mysteriously downloaded from its central computer—*"

Giles ignored the voice from the radio in the background. It was already nightfall and he had gone through a dozen books until he'd found the correct references to what he needed. "Binding ritual," he murmured. "There we are." Now if he could only—

"Hi," Jenny Calendar said from behind him. "I got your message. What's so urgent?"

Giles sat back. "Thank you for coming. I need your help. But before that, um, I need you to believe something that you may not want to." He took a deep breath, wishing he could speed up time and just be past the awkward part. "Something," he began, "has gotten into the . . . uh, inside . . ." He looked at her wordlessly for a second, then simply blurted it out.

"There's a demon in the Internet."

Incredibly, Ms. Calendar neither laughed nor walked away. She said simply, "I know."

Giles's expression drained into genuine concern as Ms. Calendar smiled slightly, turned without saying anything, then pulled the door to the library closed.

Buffy was frantic by the time they clambered up the steps to Willow's front porch. It didn't help that the door swung open, unlocked, when she started to knock.

Xander blanched. "This isn't good."

"Willow!" Buffy yelled. Without waiting, she hurried inside and up the stairs, beelining for her pal's room. "Willow?"

"Okay," Xander said from behind her when they realized the room was empty. "Any thoughts?"

Buffy's gaze stopped on the computer and the message that had come up, obviously from Malcolm.

NO MORE WAITING. I NEED YOU TO SEE ME.

"See him how?" she asked. "And where?"

Xander raised an eyebrow. "How about CRD?"

"The research place?"

He nodded. "I'm guessing that's Moloch Central."

"I suppose it's our best lead." She glanced back at the screen with a frown. "Let's just hope Giles can back us up."

No more waiting, Buffy thought. *You got that right.*

She grabbed Xander's sleeve and they raced out of Willow's house.

* * *

Giles stood, very slowly, his gaze never moving away from Jenny Calendar. He resisted the urge to take a step back, unwilling to reveal his fear. "You already know," he repeated. "How exactly is that?"

"Come on—there've been portents for days. Power surges, on-line shutdowns—you should see the bones I've been casting!" She moved back and forth across the floor, her hands fluttering with excitement. "I *knew* this would happen sooner or later! It's probably a mischief demon—you know, like Kelkor, or—"

"It's Moloch," Giles put in.

Ms. Calendar stopped and stared at him. "The Corruptor? Oh boy." Realization slid over her face. "I should have remembered—"

Giles raised a hand to his temple, unable to stop himself from squeezing his eyes shut momentarily. "You don't seem exactly surprised by— Who *are* you?"

A small smile played at the corner of Jenny Calendar's mouth. "I teach computer science at the local high school."

Giles frowned. "A profession that hardly lends itself to the casting of bones."

Ms. Calendar sent him a smug glance. "Wrong and wrong, snobby. You think the realm of the mystical is limited to ancient texts and relics? That bad old science made the magic go away?" She lifted her chin and did a fair impression of the way Giles knew he sometimes looked. "The divine exists in cyberspace same as out here."

Giles squinted at her. "Are you a witch?"

"I don't have that kind of power," she said flatly. "Technopagan is the term. There're more of us than you'd think."

He gawked at her for a moment longer, but a moment was all he could spare. Then, the book of rituals in hand, he rose and gestured for her to follow him to the computer in the library. "Well, you can definitely help me," he told her. "What's in cyberspace at the moment is less than divine. I have the binding rituals at hand, but I am completely out of my idiom."

Ms. Calendar hesitated, but only briefly. "Well, I can help . . . I think. I hope. I mean, this is my first real—do you know how he got in?"

Giles nodded. "He was . . . scanned is the term, I believe."

Her eyes widened. "And you want him back in the book. Right." She looked at the book, then at the computer. "Cool. But . . . shouldn't we make sure we've got enough ammo to—"

Giles cut her off. "There's no time. Moloch seems to have fixated on Willow. We need to get him out *now.*"

"Okay," she said, then repeated it, as though trying to reassure herself. "Okay. Minor panic, but I'm dealing. First thing is . . . what does the book say?"

Giles started to respond, then the telephone rang at the check-in desk. He snatched it up. "Buffy?"

"Yeah," Buffy said in response to Giles's nearly frantic greeting. She and Xander were standing at the telephone booth just down the street from the CRD building. In contrast to the activity earlier in the day, nothing moved there now.

His next question was another single word. "Willow?"

"Not at home," she told him, glancing cautiously around. "It looks like she was taken somewhere."

"Where are you?"

"CRD," she answered. "Whatever Moloch wants Willow for, it's probably in there."

"Ms. Calendar and I are working to get Moloch off-line." She could hear the anxiety in Giles's voice, but she had to urge him on. "Here's a tip," she told him. *"Hurry."* Without waiting for a reply, she hung up. An instant later, she was headed toward the gate with Xander at her side.

"This place is pretty heavily secured," Xander said worriedly. "How do we get in?"

"With jumping, sneaking, and the breaking of heads," Buffy said without missing a beat.

"I'll work on the sneaking," he said just as quickly.

Buffy eyed the gate, then hooked her fingers into it and began to climb. "I just hope Willow's still okay." She skimmed over the top and dropped gracefully to the concrete on the other side. Xander dove from the top of the fence right after her, executing a much poorer landing.

"Back way?" he puffed.

Buffy nodded. "Back way."

They darted across a small open area, then they were at the door. Buffy tried the knob, found it locked as expected, then reared back and kicked the thing out of their way.

With a final glance behind them, she motioned Xander to follow her inside CRD.

Willow came to lying on a steel gurney, a feeling far too close to what she imagined waking on a morgue cart might be. One long moment—*too* long—and she sat up quickly. She was in a lab of some sort, but much darker than the facilities at school and deeper in shadow. Everything she saw was made of high tech metal or plastic. As her gaze swung around, Willow finally pinpointed the door, a lighter rectangle amid the gloom.

But before she could stand and run for it, figures filled the entryway.

* * * *

WELCOME, MY LOVE.

Willow shook her head and tried to clear it. That voice—it was familiar, but not. She found her footing and turned slowly, still trying to get her bearings. Glowing in the darkness at the other end of the room was a computer terminal, and Willow finally realized who she was hearing.

I CAN'T TELL YOU HOW GOOD
IT IS TO SEE YOU—

Then, to Willow's horror, a heavy, metal hand lowered into view and rested on top of the monitor.

She didn't want to, but she had to lift her head until she saw the rest of the package it was attached to. The voice, Willow realized, hadn't come from the computer at all. Rather, it had come from this . . . *thing* stepping out of the darkness and coming toward her, a huge, horned demon, hideous to look at and made entirely of gleaming metal. A robot, complete with malevolently glowing red eyes.

—WITH MY OWN TWO EYES.

Willow stared upward. She wanted to run, to cower and hide, to do *anything* but stand here and face the awful truth. But she had no choice.

"Finally 'see' me?" she whispered in a strangled voice. She felt paralyzed, but not enough to keep the next, brutal question from coming out. *"Malcolm?"*

For a mini-eternity, no one moved or said anything. Then she tried instinctively to step back and away from the monstrosity that began slowly walking toward her. Immediately Willow found herself flanked by Fritz and a white-coated geek/scientist she'd never seen before. Moloch's digitized voice boomed through the room.

> THIS WORLD IS SO NEW, SO EXCITING.
> AND I CAN SEE ALL OF IT. EVERYTHING
> FLOWS THROUGH ME. I KNOW THE
> SECRETS OF YOUR KINGS.

The computerized demon paused and looked down at his hands, turning them over as he contemplated the way they worked.

> BUT NONE OF IT COMPARES TO HAVING FORM
> AGAIN. TO BE ABLE TO WALK. TO TOUCH.

The Malcolm monster stopped in front of her, then reached to the side with one huge hand and placed it ever so gently on Fritz's head. The young man smiled rapturously at the touch—

—and Malcolm suddenly whipped Fritz's head around, instantly snapping his neck.

> TO KILL.

The demon started to turn back toward her, then paused and cocked its massive head. Something white— a tiny light—blinked in the mass of wires and metal pieces within its horns, as though it were receiving a message from somewhere else.

> AH. HERE THEY COME.

Willow was afraid to ask what that meant.

* * *

It's a good thing it's late, Giles thought. *I wouldn't want to explain to anyone why the computer science teacher and I are lighting candles around a computer in the darkened library. Life on the Hellmouth—always challenging.*

Jenny Calendar's question pulled his attention back to the job at hand. "The first thing we have to do is form the Circle of Kayless, right?"

Giles nodded, but he was still perplexed. "Form the Circle—but there's only two of us. That's really more of a line."

"You're not getting it, Rupert." Ms. Calendar settled in front of the computer. "We have to form the Circle *inside.* I'm putting out a flash. I just hope enough of my group responds."

Concern creased Giles's forehead. "Won't Moloch just shut you down?"

"Well," she said with a determined expression, "I'm betting he won't figure out what we're doing until it's too late."

" 'Hoping' and 'betting.' That's what we've got." He stared at the computer as if his wishes could help it along.

Ms. Calendar glanced at him. "You want to throw in 'praying,' be my guest."

Fritz's body lay on the floor at the robot's feet like a sad and broken toy, and Willow edged backward, trying to put distance between her and Malcolm. One foot, one more . . . then the white-coated scientist realized what she was doing and grabbed her by the arm. Instinctively, she yanked roughly away, then glared at Malcolm. "I don't understand," she said. "What do you want from me?"

The metal demon gazed in her direction, as if it couldn't believe she didn't know.

* * *

I WANT TO GIVE YOU THE WORLD.

"Why?" Willow demanded.

Another gray metallic stare before he answered.

YOU CREATED ME. I BROUGHT THESE HUMANS
TOGETHER TO BUILD ME A BODY, BUT YOU GAVE
ME LIFE. TOOK ME OUT OF THE BOOK THAT
HELD ME. I WANT TO REPAY YOU.

Willow shook her head, fighting not to cry. "By lying to me? By pretending to be a person?" She paused, struggling even more with unshed tears. "Pretending that you *loved* me."

If the monstrosity that was Malcolm could have given her a deceitful smile, Willow was convinced it would have.

I DO.

Before she could reply, Malcolm spread his huge, clawed hands as if in supplication.

DON'T YOU SEE? I CAN GIVE YOU
EVERYTHING. I CAN CONTROL THE WORLD.

He stopped for a moment and Willow thought she could almost *see* the thought processes going on in his computerized head, the files being read and stored, the cross-referencing. His next words confirmed her suspicions.

RIGHT NOW A MAN IN BEIJING IS
TRANSFERRING MONEY TO A SWISS BANK

ACCOUNT FOR A CONTRACT ON HIS
MOTHER'S LIFE. GOOD FOR HIM.

"You're evil," Willow said flatly. But Malcolm wasn't at all perturbed by her statement.

IS THAT A PROBLEM?

* * *

Buffy marched through the hallway door and met the security guard midway. He blocked her path and reached for his weapon, but her fist made friends with his nose without her even breaking stride.

"Buffy—"

She would have automatically made for the door on the other side of the room, but Xander motioned her over to the security station. He pointed at the figures on a small video monitor built into the desk above a label that read ROBOTICS LAB 02.

"It's her!" Buffy exclaimed.

"Yeah," Xander agreed. They peered at the screen, where Willow was facing off with something else— something huge and dark and menacing. Panic edged Xander's voice. *"But who's the other guy?"*

Without trying to answer, Buffy sprinted for the door. Inside were stairs and it wasn't hard to follow the signs to the second floor, although having to read the directions fired her impatience to find Willow. Finally they burst into the room adjoining where they wanted to be, but when Buffy yanked on the handle to the door marked ROBOTICS LAB 02, she found it solidly locked. She hammered on it with her fists, then stepped back in frustration.

"I can't bust this," she told Xander. "It's heavy steel."

Xander looked frantically around. "Then let's find another way in—"

His words stopped short when the lights went out, leaving only a few emergency bulbs to cast a dim, eerie glow around them. A sound—*K-CHUNK!*—made Xander rush back to the door through which they'd come; it was now firmly secured, probably by a hidden deadbolt mechanism.

"What's going on?" he demanded.

Buffy spied a security camera high in one corner and pointed to it. "The building's security system is computerized!"

Xander swallowed. "Whoops." As he stared upward, he saw a small, electrical indicator marked FIRE next to the camera blink to sudden life.

And streams of a poisonous fire extinguisher chemical began pumping into the room.

"Almost there," Jenny Calendar said. A worldwide map was splayed across the computer screen in front of her, and on it was a line running from Sunnydale to various cities around the world. Point to point, they blinked to form a global circle.

Giles frowned at it. "Couldn't you just stop Moloch by entering some computer virus?"

"You've seen way too many movies," she said without taking her eyes from the screen. "Okay—we're up!" Now she did turn to him, her expression all business. "You read, I type. Ready?"

"I am," Giles answered.

Ms. Calendar spit lightly into one palm, then rubbed her hands together before poising them over the keys.

Giles cleared his throat and began reciting the ancient binding ritual. "By the power of the divine," he intoned. Jenny Calendar typed rapidly, keeping up with every word. "By the essence of the word. I command you—"

* * *

In the robotics lab, Willow jumped as something banged hard against the door behind Malcolm, then banged again. Who was out there—maybe Buffy? Who else could find a way into this place, make it past the robot demon's goons? But the pounding on the door was weakening with every strike, and Malcolm seemed content to just stand and listen. This gave her a bad, bad feeling about things.

"What are you doing?" Willow demanded.

WHAT COMES NATURALLY.

Naturally? Of course—and hadn't she just said only moments ago that he was evil? Who knew what he was causing in the other room. "Let me leave," Willow begged.

BUT I LOVE YOU.

The sound of that metallic voice uttering those special words nearly made Willow break down. "Don't say that! That's a *joke*—you don't love *anything*!"

YOU . . . ARE MINE.

Her face twisted in anger and regret, Willow stood her ground as he stepped toward her. "I'm not yours—I'm never gonna *be* yours. Never!"

That seemed to make Malcolm pause. He lowered his heavy, horned head, but she couldn't tell if it was because she'd hurt him or he was simply considering his next move. After a moment, he lifted his chin and the light pulsed behind his red eyes.

PITY. I'LL MISS YOU.

When he grabbed her head, his speed was much more terrifying than Willow had expected. A vision filled her mind, a flashback of what Malcolm had done to poor, misguided Fritz only minutes ago.

Willow was screaming even before his fingers began to tighten.

Giles's voice was filled with righteous power, one hand gesturing as he recited the ritual. "By the power of the Circle of Kayless, I command you!" He paused for a moment and looked at the screen, then back to Ms. Calendar. "Kayless. With a 'K.'"

Ms. Calendar stabbed at the erase key. "Right. Sorry."

Giles looked back at his book and took a deep breath. "Demon, *COME!*"

In the midst of her scream, Malcolm suddenly let her go.

He reared back as if someone had looped an invisible chain around his neck and pulled, and his own bellow—long and harsh—cut through the room. Willow heard a clanking sound beneath it, like a door unbolting. There was another pounding, and suddenly the door behind Malcolm flew open. Buffy staggered through amid a dissipating cloud of something chemical, dragging a nearly senseless Xander.

"Buffy!" Willow cried.

Malcolm reached for her again and Buffy pushed Xander to the side, drew herself up, and launched into a flying kick straight at the center of Malcolm's stomach.

The robot demon tottered backward but maintained its balance. "Ow!" Buffy exclaimed as she thumped to the floor. "Guy's made of metal!" Behind Buffy, Willow saw the lab guy grab Xander and haul him off his feet. Buffy yanked her toward the door, but not before Malcolm saw them and planted his hulking robot form in front of them. His arms stretched out, then he clutched his head and screamed again.

NO! I WON'T GO BACK—!

* * *

The library computer hummed and suddenly popped, sending a shower of sparks over the keyboard as the screen flashed.

"Whoa!" Ms. Calendar said and scooted backward.

"I COMMAND YOU!" Giles bellowed.

Not one to give up easily, Ms. Calendar squared her shoulders, leaned over and banged out the words on the keyboard, ignoring the sparks and the whirlwind of colors now streaming across the screen. She hit the ENTER key with a solid *thwack!* and a sort of cosmic boom filled the library, swirling around her and Giles with nearly tornado force.

Then it was over, and the screen went dark.

"It worked!" Ms. Calendar said triumphantly. "He's out of the net. He's bound!"

Giles blinked at the screen, then reached for the anti-quated leather-bound volume and flipped it open.

"He's not in the book," Giles said slowly.

Ms. Calendar's eyes were huge and she hurried over. "He's not in the book?" Then she saw the creamy, blank expanse of the old pages. *"Where is he?"*

As she and Buffy scurried through the lab door, Willow saw Xander throw himself backward and smash the lab guy into the wall. The guy let go and Xander spun and gave him an admirable punch full in the stomach. He was back with them before the man fell all the way to the floor. "I got to hit someone!" he said, looking absurdly proud.

Neither she nor Buffy commented as they made for a door farther down the hall. They were right on top of it when it swung open, revealing the security guard from the first floor with two more scientist-types for backup. Before the uninvited trio could come through, Buffy slammed the door shut again and twisted the lock below the knob.

Xander tugged at Buffy's arm. "Let's go this way!" He sprinted in the other direction.

Buffy looked at Willow. "Wait!" she called. Suddenly the entire wall in front of them literally *exploded* as an enraged Malcolm smashed through it. It turned its head, saw Xander when he spun back, and backhanded the boy. Willow screamed as the robot grabbed Buffy, then tossed her against the other wall as though she were made of nothing but feathers. Stunned, she slid down and didn't move.

There was no denying the robot demon was furious. His eyes were burning coals, and when he spoke, his voice was black thunder, sinking into their eardrums like shards of steel.

I WAS OMNIPOTENT! I WAS EVERYTHING!
NOW I'M TRAPPED IN THIS SHELL!

Still dazed, Willow realized that all Buffy could do was wait as Malcolm's terrible clawed hand reached for her. *I have to do something!*

"Malcolm!"

The metal monster turned at the sound of Willow's voice. She'd seen the oversized fire extinguisher on the wall and now she hefted it, then smashed it into his head as hard as she could.

"Remember me?" Willow demanded through gritted teeth. "Your *girlfriend?*"

Before Malcolm could recover, she swung the fire extinguisher again—

"I'm thinking we should break up!"

—and again.

"But maybe we can still be *friends.*"

She tried to swing a fourth time, but Malcolm knocked it out of her hands, then hit her. She went sailing through the air and crashed into Xander as he tried to stand.

Malcolm swung back to Buffy. Untangling herself, Willow saw her friend wobble upright, then automatically punch the robot in the stomach.

Bad idea.

"Ahhhh!" Buffy yelled, backing up and shaking her bruised hand. The Malcolm robot matched her step for step. His next words were filled with evil intent.

THIS BODY IS ALL I HAVE LEFT,
BUT IT'S ENOUGH TO CRUSH YOU.

Dismayed, Willow realized that Malcolm had now backed Buffy into a corner—there was no escape. Then she saw Buffy glance behind her and focus on something: a huge, high voltage breaker box right above her shoulder. She took a final backward step and grinned at the monster.

"Take your best shot," Buffy said sweetly.

Willow wanted to scrunch her eyes shut and not see what was about to happen, but she couldn't. Again she knew that if metal robots could smile, this one would have. Malcolm drew back his gleaming fist and drove it toward her best friend's face with everything he had—

—and Buffy ducked.

Malcolm's punch slammed into the breaker box. The smell of electrical current filled the room as mini flashes of lightning zipped over and around Malcolm's robot form. He shook violently and took a step toward Buffy as smoke and sparks poured from his eyes. His heavy jaw quivered but no sound came out.

Buffy didn't wait around. "Get *down!*" she screamed and dove to the floor next to Willow and Xander.

The sound of Malcolm exploding filled Willow's head and made her teeth ache. When the smoke finally cleared, all she could do was sit with her friends and stare at her boyfriend's lifeless, metal-sheathed head.

EPILOGUE

"**W**ell," Jenny Calendar said with a smile as she saw him come into the computer lab the next day. "Look who's here. Welcome to my world. You scared?"

Giles smiled slightly. The Calendar woman did have a dry sense of humor, and he couldn't help but admire that. "I'm remaining calm, thank you. I just wanted to return this." He held up a strange little earring that resembled a corkscrew. "I found it among the new books and naturally I thought of you."

"Cool," she said, reaching for it. "Thanks."

He turned to go, but stopped at her next words.

"Listen, you're not planning to mention our little . . . adventure, are you? To anyone on the school staff?"

Giles raised an eyebrow. "Nothing could be further from my mind."

"Great," Ms. Calendar said, relieved. "Pagan rituals and magic spells tend to freak the administration."

He nodded. "Yes, I know. I'll see you." This time he made it a whole two steps.

"Can't get out of here fast enough, can you?"

Giles faced her again. "Truthfully, I'm even less anxious to be around computers than I used to be."

Ms. Calendar made a final tap on her computer keyboard, then stood. "Well, it was *your* book that started the trouble, not a computer. Honestly, what is it about them that bothers you so much?"

He hesitated, then decided to be truthful. After all, that's what she'd asked for. "The smell."

She looked completely puzzled. "Computers don't smell, Rupert."

"I know," he said. He stepped over to a table and lifted a couple of school textbooks, fingering the binding and covers. "Smell is the most powerful memory trigger there is. A certain flower or a whiff of smoke can bring up experiences long forgotten. Books smell—musty and rich. The knowledge gained from a computer has no . . . texture, no context. It's there and then it's gone." He placed the books back on the table almost regretfully. "If it's to last, then the getting of knowledge should be tangible. It should be *smelly*."

They looked at each other, then a slow smile spread across Jenny Calendar's face and her eyes sparkled. "You really are an old-fashioned boy, aren't you?"

"Well," Giles said, suddenly feeling a bit flustered. "It's true I don't dangle a corkscrew from my ear."

Her smile went just a touch mischievous. "That's . . . not where it dangles."

Ms. Calendar turned and strolled away, leaving Giles to stare after her, his mouth in an *O* of surprise and his mind filled with reluctant curiosity.

* * *

The sun was shining, the Malcolm/Moloch demon was dead, and she and her friends were all still alive. She should have felt great, but overall, Willow was pretty glum.

"So," Xander said. He gave her a patented goofy-Xander grin. "We gonna go to the Bronze tonight? We three?"

On her other side, Buffy smiled. "It'll be fun."

When Willow didn't say anything, Xander tried again. "Willow? Fun? Remember fun? That thing where you smile?"

She shrugged and stared at her books. "I'm sorry, guys. I'm just thinking about . . ."

Buffy looked at her knowingly. "Malcolm?"

She nodded. "Malcolm. Moloch. Whatever he's called. The one boy that's really liked me and he's a demon robot." She looked sadly at her friends. "What does that say about me?"

"It doesn't say anything about you," Buffy said.

Willow shook her head. "I mean . . . I thought I was really falling—"

Buffy put a hand on her arm. "Hey, did you forget? The one boy I've had the hots for here turned out to be a vampire."

"Right!" Xander cut in enthusiastically. "And the teacher *I* had a crush on? Giant praying mantis."

"That's true!" Willow said, brightening. So, really, she wasn't the only one who'd gotten fooled.

"It's life on the Hellmouth," Xander said, and Willow knew there was no arguing about that.

"Let's face it," Buffy said cheerfully. "None of us are ever going to have a happy, normal relationship."

Xander laughed. "We're doomed!"

Willow nodded and gave them a happy smile. "Yeah!"

For a few seconds all three of them looked at one another and giggled. Then everything they'd just said sunk into their minds and took hold.

Their laughter sputtered out and Willow found herself sitting with her two best friends once again, glum, while they all contemplated the future.

DAILY JOURNAL ENTRY:

```
It's been a long time since that awful
night at CRD, but sometimes I still
think about . . . well . . .
    Malcolm.
    I mean, not the Moloch-infested Mal-
colm. The "good" Malcolm—the one the
demon invented to get to me. He did a
good job, and I was so ready to ditch
some really important parts of my life
for him. My schoolwork, my friends, who
knows what else. I can't believe I al-
most did that—it's a good thing I dis-
covered the truth in time.
    And so much else has happened since
then! I've been keeping my journal en-
tries up to date, sure. But I thought
it was time for a kind of report on all
the Sunnydale action—how it's affected
me and my best friends in the world,
Buffy and Xander. Sometimes a person
has to step back and take stock—see
where she is, where she's going. You
know, so the future—and it's always an
adventure on the Hellmouth—doesn't grab
her from behind.
```

Okay. From where I see it, everything seems to revolve around the hunt for a partner. Girls want a boyfriend, boys want a girlfriend. Even the old adults, like Giles and Buffy's mom, Joyce Summers, haven't given up the hunt. Mrs. Summers had a terrible experience with that Ted guy who turned out to be a robot (there's familiar territory!). But Giles seems to be, you know, doing okay with Ms. Calendar. So it's like this: Sunnydale's full of vampires and demons and all sorts of yucky monsters...but the majority of them want the same thing. I mean, other than the essential stuff like blood and brains to eat, lots of money, or to be noticed, sure. But the rest...

Take a look around if you think I'm nuts—it's all right there. Even Buffy isn't immune to it. That so showed in the way she acted while trying to make Angel jealous after she died and Xander revived her. It's totally painful to see how heartbroken she is now that Angel's gone...well, *bad*. And when that boy from her old school, Billy Fordham, turned out to only be using her to try to get immortality? I thought that was the saddest I could ever see her. I guess I was wrong.

Poor Xander—he got hurt, too, when he fell for Ampata, that South American exchange student who was really a soul-sucking Incan princess. That was twice for him, with that praying mantis teacher the first time. Now, gag me! He's dating Cordelia, of all people. I never would've thought she'd end up a Slayerette like the rest of us. And all because she and Xander met that nasty bug-man, Mr. Pfister, when Spike sent The Order of Taraka after Buffy. Gee, could it be that Xander's going for the three-strikes-you're-out award?

Okay, I admit it—I'm jealous. I mean, I *was* jealous. But I'm not anymore. At least . . . I don't think I am. I can't be, right? It just stung so majorly to realize that he wanted Cordelia instead of me. Yeah, she's beautiful but also utterly brainless. And does she ever have a nice thing to say to *anyone*? *Not*. And please—Cordelia is completely the queen of the Significant Other Search. Still, her regularly scheduled stomp on her Boy-Of-The-Week got a shot of shock when Daryl Epps tried to make her his eternity partner.

So Xander's always having these crushes on everything wearing a skirt. I mean, he's a guy, what can you expect? But ever since we were little, I . . . well, I always thought Xander would end up with me. But then . . .

Well, then came Oz.

He's cute and as smart as me—which is good because at least I feel like I'm having a conversation with a guy who thinks about something *other* than the length of my dress. It was so excellent—when he found out about the vampires and other nasties in Sunnydale when we were trying to stop Spike from reconstructing the Judge? Didn't freak him out a bit. And he's totally considerate and sensitive—I can't believe I tried to get him to make out with me just to get back at Xander for Cordelia. But Oz saw right through that and turned me down—and I could tell that it was because he wanted me. I mean, wanted me to be interested in him because he was Oz, not . . . never mind. He's right, of course; way too many people around here are big on using one person to get to someone else. That is so not cool, and I'm ashamed I even thought about it.

But the thing about Oz is that he's *too* cautious. I mean . . . I'm interested, he's interested. He has the *look*. There are some things a girl can just tell.

So why doesn't Oz just go on and . . . do something about it?

/Press Enter To Save File/

FILE: PHASES

PROLOGUE

Willow caught up with Oz in the main hallway. Despite the noise and near chaos of the start of the Sunnydale High school day, he was bending forward and intently studying something inside one of the trophy cases. When she stepped up next to him, his smile made her cheeks feel pleasantly warm. "Hi."

"That's what I was going to say." Oz looked at her, then glanced back at the case, still fascinated by something inside.

"Whatcha looking at?"

"This cheerleader trophy," he answered, pointing at it. "It's like its eyes follow you wherever you go." Watching it carefully, he leaned first to one side, then the other. Then he smiled again. "I like it."

He straightened, then began to walk with Willow as she angled toward the main hallway and her locker.

"So," she said after a moment, "did you like the movie last night?"

He shrugged. "I don't know. Today's movies are kind of like popcorn. You know, you forget about them as soon as they're done. I do remember I liked the popcorn though."

"Yeah," she agreed. "It was good. And I had a really fun time at the rest. I mean," she paused, trying not to fumble, "the part with you."

That got her another unique Oz-like smile as they came to a juncture in the hallway. "Well, that's great, because my time was also of the good."

"Mine, too." This was it, the point where he'd have to go one way and she the other. *Will he kiss me good-bye?*

"Well, then . . ." *Darn it, it isn't happening.* The silence stretched as they looked at each other, but the two feet between them might as well have been the width of Revello Drive. She needed an escape, and when she glanced around, Buffy was the object of convenience.

"Oh, there! I have . . . my friend. So I will go to her."

"I'll see you, then," Oz said easily. "Later."

Face burning, hoping she wasn't actually *red*, Willow hurried off to join Buffy down the hall.

Still smiling slightly, Oz watched her go. As he did, something blocked his vision and he found himself face to face with Larry, a bruiser of a jock who always had a pack of Larryettes following him around. "Man, Oz," Larry said, leering in the direction of Willow and Buffy. "I would *love* to get me some of that Buffy and Willow action, if you know what I mean."

Oz raised an eyebrow. "That's great, Larry. You've really mastered the single entendre."

Larry looked at him blankly, then his attention switched to a good-looking blond girl strolling past.

Quicker than Oz could have considered it, Larry reached out and "accidentally" sent her books tumbling groundward. "Oops," Larry said with all the emotion of a cactus.

"Hey!" Larry's victim sent him a revolted look as she bent to retrieve her things, but Larry was anything but concerned.

"Thank you, Thighmaster!" he hooted as he and his cohorts leaned in to enjoy the view. *Brainless,* Oz thought ruefully. Perhaps not, as that might imply they'd had brains to begin with.

The girl stomped off and Larry turned back to Oz. "So, Oz, man, what's up with that?" Larry posed in what Oz assumed was supposed to be a manly position. "Dating a junior? Let me guess—that little innocent schoolgirl thing is just an act, right?"

Oz nodded wisely. "Yeah. Yeah, she's actually an evil Mastermind. It's fun."

The humor was wasted. "I mean, she's gotta be putting out, or what's the point? What are you gonna do, *talk?*" Larry grinned like a fool and rolled his eyes. "Come on, 'fess up. How far have you got?"

Oz sighed and wondered just how long he could go on with the Mastermind story before the brain-challenged jock would realize it was a put-on.

"Nowhere!" Willow said, and it was all she could do not to wave her books around. "I mean, he said he was gonna wait until I was ready, but I'm ready! Honest—I'm good to go here!"

Buffy rested her chin on her fist. "I think it's nice he's not just being an animal."

"It *is* nice," Willow agreed. "He's great. We have a lot of fun. But I want smoochies!"

"Have you dropped any hints?" Buffy asked.

"I've dropped anvils."

"He'll come around," Buffy told her. "What guy could resist your wily, Willow charms?"

Willow frowned. "At last count? All of them. Maybe more."

Buffy gave a rebellious shake of her head. "Well, none of them know a thing. They all get an *F* in Willow."

"But I want Oz to get an *A*. And, oh—" She brightened as she turned to face her friend. "And one of those gold stars!"

They stopped for a while and sat beneath a tree. "He will," Buffy said confidently.

"Well, he'd better hurry." Willow was sulking, and she knew it, but it felt right. "I don't want to be the only girl in school without a real boyfriend—"

The words were out before she could stop them, and when she saw Buffy staring at her lap, Willow just wanted to smack herself. "Oh, I'm such an idiot—I'm sorry. I shouldn't even be talking about . . ." She hesitated. "Do you want me to go away?"

"I wish you wouldn't," Buffy said quietly.

Another hesitation, but what kind of a friend would she be if she didn't ask? "How are you holding up, anyway?"

"I'm holding." Buffy looked at her ruefully. "I was going on close to two minutes there without thinking about Angel."

"Well," Willow said as cheerfully as she could. "There you go!"

Buffy gave her a brave smile. "But I'd be doing a lot better if you and Xander and I could do that 'sharing our misery' thing tonight."

"Great." Willow looked at her friend from beneath lowered eyelids. "I'll give Xander a call, ask him to join us. What's his number? Oh, yeah—1-800-I'm-Dating-A-Skanky-Ho."

Buffy's eyes widened in surprise. "Me-*ow!*"

Willow was pleased. "Really? Thanks—I've never gotten a 'me-ow' before."

This time Buffy laughed. "Well deserved."

"Darn tootin'!" Willow made a dismissive sound and gathered up her books. "I'm just saying, Xander and *Cordelia?* What does he see in her, anyway?"

Hours later, with the day's school problems behind them, Xander and Cordelia were parked in a nice, private spot in Makeout Park. It was a warm night with a gentle breeze, and amid the lushness of the leafy trees, the sky was split by stars and bright moonlight. Between the two teenagers, the kisses were coming hot and heavy—

—then Xander pulled away.

"But what could she possibly see in him?"

Cordelia threw up her hands in exasperation. "Excuse me? We did not come here to talk about Willow." She gave Xander a hard look. "We came here to do things I can never tell my father about because he still thinks I'm a good girl."

"I just don't trust Oz with her," Xander said, totally zoning past her irritation. "I mean, he's a senior, he's attractive. Okay, not to me, but . . . Oh, and he's in a band. And we know what element that kind attracts."

Cordelia sat back. "I've dated lots of guys in bands."

"Thank you!" Xander said pointedly.

She stared at him. "Do you even *want* to be here?"

Xander blinked. "I'm not running away."

"Because when you're not babbling about poor, defenseless Willow," she said, "you are *raving* about the all-powerful Buffy."

"I do not babble," Xander said huffily. "I occasionally run on. And every now and then I yammer—"

"Xander, look around," Cordelia interrupted with exaggerated gentleness. "We're in my daddy's car. It's just the two of us. There is a beautiful, big full moon. It doesn't get any more romantic than this. So shut *up!*" She grabbed him and yanked him forward.

Xander didn't protest. But they were in the middle of a really good smooch when instinct made him pull back anyway.

"Did you hear that?" he asked, peering out the window.

"What is it now?" Cordelia demanded impatiently.

Xander frowned out at the shadowy park. "I thought I heard something."

This time, Cordelia's voice was thick with sarcasm. "Is Willow sending some sort of distress signal that only you can hear?"

Xander ignored the jibe and glanced outside again. Nothing. "Huh," he said. He leaned toward Cordelia and she came to him willingly, but before their lips could meet he jolted back again. "Okay, now I *know* I heard something."

Cordelia twisted angrily away. "All right, that's it. Your mind has been not here all night. How 'bout I just drop you off at—"

Something punched a hole right through the leather top of the convertible.

They both screamed, long and loud, as a huge, claw-tipped paw swiped into the space between the seats, right where they'd faced each other only seconds before. It was there, then it was gone; when they looked again, peering at them through the slashed top was a hairy, snouted face and a snarling mouth that seemed to contain a thousand teeth—

Werewolf!

"Get us out of here!" Xander shouted as the creature groped through the hole again.

"Where are the *keys?*" Cordelia shrieked. She ducked down and her fingertips scrabbled across the floorboard as the car rocked around her. Still searching, she caught a glimpse of Xander, shoving himself against the door to stay out of reach of the beast's claws. "We should be moving!" he yelled. "Let's *go!*"

She felt cool metal and snatched at it. "Got 'em!" An instant later she jammed them into the ignition and sent up a silent thanks as the engine fired on the first try. She threw the transmission into reverse and hit the accelerator, spinning the wheel as the werewolf growled and clung to the remains of the convertible top. Then she slammed on the brakes and yanked the gearshift into drive; she floored it and the car shot forward. The werewolf snarled and lost its grip, and they left it howling and lying in the dirt as they raced off into the night.

Xander had to say it. He couldn't *not.*

"Told you I heard something."

CHAPTER 1

It was hard to believe the horrors of last night.

Until Willow and the rest of the gang looked at Cordelia's car parked in the school's lot.

"And you're sure it was a werewolf?" Buffy asked, fingering the slashed material.

"Well, let's see," Xander replied. "Six feet tall, claws, a big ol' snout right in the middle of a face like a wolf." He sent her a severe look. "Yeah, I'm sticking with my first guess."

"Seems wise," Oz agreed.

Willow saw Xander make a mock, I-almost-forgot face. "Oh, and there was that little thing where it tried to *bite* us."

That made Cordelia bury her head in Xander's shoulder. "It was so awful."

"I know," Xander said soothingly, and Willow had to admit that even she felt a pang of sympathy for Cordy.

Cordelia raised her head. "Daddy just had this car detailed!"

Never mind.

Giles had been standing a little way off, studying a newspaper. Now he joined them. "So what's the word?" Buffy asked when she saw him unfold it.

The librarian showed them the headlines. "Seems there were a number of other attacks by a 'wild dog' around town. Several animal carcasses were found mutilated."

Willow's eyes widened. "Oh, you mean bunnies and stuff?" Before anyone could answer, she shook her head. "No, don't tell me."

Oz looked at Willow. "Oh, don't worry. They may not look it, but bunnies can really take care of themselves."

"Yeah," Willow said. While the words were ridiculous, she still found them comforting.

Giles pressed his lips together. "Yes. Well, fortunately, no *people* were injured."

Buffy looked surprised. "That falls into the 'that's a switch' column."

Giles nodded. "For now. But my guess is this werewolf will be back at next month's full moon."

"What about *tonight's* full moon?" Willow asked pointedly.

Giles blinked. "Pardon?"

"Last night was the night before the full moon," Willow explained. "Traditionally known as . . . the night before the full moon."

Giles frowned. "Meaning the accepted legend that werewolves only prowl during the full moon might be erroneous."

"Or it could be a crock," Cordelia said.

Xander nodded. "Unless the werewolf is still using last year's almanac."

"Looks like Giles has some schoolin' to do," Buffy noted.

Giles nodded a little too enthusiastically. "Yes, I must admit I'm intrigued. A werewolf? It's one of the classics. I'm sure my books and I are in for a fascinating afternoon."

Willow and the others watched him hurry off. When she looked at Buffy, her friend only shrugged. "He needs to get a pet."

The voices of a full class of students laughing and talking echoed through the gymnasium. They all sat in the lower rows of the stands, watching as Ms. Litto, looking strong and capable, strode across the floor in front of them. Sitting with her pals, Willow had listened to the Phys Ed teacher talk with dismay, realizing that she had clearly arranged the lesson plan for this class because of the recent attacks.

"Sunnydale is becoming more dangerous all the time. And a full moon like tonight tends to bring out the crazies. *But,* with some simple basics of self-defense, each of you can learn how to protect yourself," Ms. Litto told them.

"Here's a suggestion," Buffy muttered beside Willow. "Move away from the Hellmouth."

From behind her, Oz suddenly reached forward and did something tickly to the back of Willow's neck. "Tag," he explained when she turned toward him.

Willow barely registered Xander's complaint, uttered from the other side of Buffy and Cordelia. "Would you look at that? He's all over her!" Suddenly he leaned in front of the other two girls. "Hey buddy," he said to Oz in a false whisper, "this is a public forum here!"

Cordelia shot Xander a disgusted glance as the rest of them looked at him, bewildered. "I think you splashed on a little too much 'Obsession for Dorks.' "

Ms. Litto clapped her hands. "Okay, everyone get into your assigned groups."

The guys got up and began stripping off sweatshirts and sweaters and putting on body pads, but they were still close enough for Willow to hear what was going on with Oz. Getting ready with him were Xander and Larry. The jock slipped off his jacket to reveal a bandage wrapped around one elbow.

Xander eyed the dressing. "What happened to you?"

Larry looked irritated. "Ah, last week some huge dog jumped out of the bushes and bit me—thirty-nine stitches. They ought to shoot those strays."

"I been there, man." Oz held up a finger wrapped with a Band-Aid. "My cousin Jordy. Just got his grown-up teeth in, does *not* like to be tickled."

Willow leaned in to see. "Looks like it healed already."

Oz gave her a slight smile. "The emotional scar is still there."

Larry turned away, then sauntered up to Theresa, a small, pretty girl with dark hair. "Theresa!" he said jovially. "Be still my shorts. We're in the same group." His face held just a shade of cruelty. "I may have to attack you."

Theresa looked around anxiously. "No, I think, actually, in our group there're a few of us—"

Buffy cut in with obvious anticipation and a sugary smile for Larry. "And I'm one of the few."

Theresa backed out of harm's way as Willow snagged Buffy's arm and pulled her aside. "Don't forget," she reminded Buffy urgently. "You're supposed to be a meek little girlie-girl like the rest of us."

She let go and saw Buffy pout briefly. "Spoil my fun." Still, she went back to Larry and tried her best to look attackable.

Xander suddenly waltzed past her and Cordelia, grinning foolishly as he pulled a large, padded helmet over his head. "Be gentle with me."

Cordelia looked at Willow. "You first," she said, her voice barely above a sneer. "I wouldn't want to be accused of taking your place in line."

Willow raised an eyebrow. "Oh, I think you pushed your way to the front long before this."

Cordelia shrugged prettily. "Hey, I can't help it if I get the spotlight just because some people blend into the background."

Willow felt her teeth clench at the insult. "Well, maybe some people could see better if you weren't standing on the auction block, shaking your wares."

"Sorry. We haven't all perfected that phony 'girl next door' bit."

"You could be the girl next door, too," Willow snapped. "If Xander lived next to a brothel!" *Ow,* Willow thought. *Did I really say that?*

Oh, but she had, and by the dark expression on Cordelia's face she knew she'd finally gotten a claw in. They took a step toward each other, but the moment was broken when Xander called out innocently, "Okay, who wants a piece of me?"

She and Cordelia gazed at each other, then turned as one to face him. Without warning, Cordelia let loose with a great cross punch to Xander's padded jaw, and Willow followed it with an excellently timid sidekick right in the center of his body armor. Cordelia moved in again, then Willow, and in no time at all, they had Xander rolled into a pathetic heap on the gym floor.

"Why . . . ?" he managed to ask, but she and Cordelia only smiled in satisfaction and turned away as Ms. Litto called out to the class to line up in pairs, one in front of the other.

"Okay, everyone. Listen up." She walked the length of the line, checking the couples as Willow zipped into the spot in front of Oz. "I want to show you what to do should you be attacked from behind."

From her place a couple of students away, Willow saw Buffy paired with Larry. *Uh-oh,* she thought, and tried to send her friend a mental reminder. *Girlie-girl, Buffy! Girlie-girl!*

"In this situation," Ms. Litto instructed as Larry wrapped one beefy arm around Buffy's neck and held her waist with the other, "bend forward, using your back and shoulders to flip your assailant over to the ground."

Ms. Litto moved on down the line of students, making sure everyone understood. Watching Buffy from the corner of her eye, Willow saw her friend pulling against Larry's arm and making spineless little "Uh! Mm-uh!" sounds as she tried vainly to flip him forward. She felt Oz start to position himself, but before she could enjoy the fact that his arm was across her collarbone, Willow heard Larry's voice drift down the line of teenagers. A chill ran across her neck at his words.

"Oh Summers, you are turning me *on!*" From the way Buffy jerked and the look on her face, Willow had no doubt that idiot-Larry had reached down and grabbed her butt.

Big mistake.

Without hesitation, Buffy bent and easily heaved Larry over her shoulder. He landed flat on his back with enough force to shake the gym floor, and there was Buffy, standing over him in her fighting stance and with her fists balled.

Oz leaned around from where Willow was trying to flip him and glanced down at Larry as everyone else in the gym also turned to stare.

"That works, too," he said blandly.

* * *

The library again, and Willow's favorite place. Even though they had talked about so many bad things here, she felt there was an inherent goodness to it, to being surrounded by all the wonderful books and history. Now Giles was using a globe, a smaller model of the moon, and a lamp for lighting as he explained the lunar phases to them.

"And while there's absolutely no scientific explanation for lunar effect on the human psyche," he continued as he moved the moon-model around the globe, "the phases of the moon seem to exert a great deal of psychological influence. And a full moon tends to bring out our darkest qualities."

Xander nodded, as if giving his approval to Giles's words. "And yet ironically, it led to the invention of the Moon Pie."

Willow and Buffy glared at Xander but amazingly, Giles began to chuckle. "Moon Pie . . ." *Did he really find that funny?* Willow thought the Watcher must be under more stress than they realized.

At their expressions, Giles cleared his throat and looked embarrassed. "You see," he said, "the werewolf is such a potent, extreme representation of our inborn animalistic traits that it emerges for three full consecutive nights—the full moon, and the two nights surrounding it."

"Quite the party animal," Willow commented.

"Quite," Giles agreed. "And it acts on pure instinct, no conscience. Predatory and aggressive—"

Buffy sat back. "In other words, your typical male."

Xander frowned. "On behalf of my gender—*hey!*"

"Yes, let's not jump to conclusions—" Giles began.

"I did not jump," Buffy said with a perfectly expressionless face. "I took a tiny step. And there conclusions were."

"The point is," Giles said, "our wolfman could also be a wolfwoman. Or anyone who was bitten by a werewolf."

Xander looked at his watch. "And whoever it is will be changing at any moment."

Willow nodded, reached over to the globe, and gave it a gentle push. It turned about halfway, as if knowing her next words. " 'Cause it'll be night soon."

"So then," Xander said, clasping his hands in summation. "I'm guessing your standard issue silver bullets are in order here?"

Giles shook his head emphatically. "No. No bullets. No matter who this werewolf is, it's still a human being who may be completely unaware of his, or her, condition."

Willow saw Buffy's eyes meet Giles's. "So," she said, "tonight we bring 'em back alive."

Makeout Park at night, and Buffy wandered quietly among the bushes at the edge of the parking lot. She could see Giles prowling between the cars, every now and then thoughtlessly shining a flashlight inside a window. *He's lucky he doesn't get popped in the nose,* she thought as she hefted her bag of supplies for the night's hunt.

Finally, they crossed paths between two of the darkened cars. "Anything yet?" Giles asked.

"Yes," Buffy whispered excitedly. "And you won't believe what I saw! Cortney Podell was making out with Owen Sadeel—but *she* goes with Barrett Woods. If he ever finds out—" Her words sputtered away as she realized what he'd meant. *Oops.* "No," she amended. "No sign of the werewolf. How about you?"

"The same," Giles said, studying the cars. "I thought we might knock on a few windows, ask if anyone's seen anything yet."

Buffy gaped at him, completely appalled. "Giles? No one's seen anything."

His mouth opened, then closed. "Oh ... yes. Of course not."

Buffy left him to roam through the parking lot and headed back into the wooded area around the lot's edge. She was barely a few yards into the bushes when she thought she heard something, so she went in deeper, stepping cautiously between the greenery. In the shadows ahead, a shape caught her eye but she couldn't quite make it out. She aimed for it, crossing out of the trees and into a small clearing—

Her feet snapped out from under her and the ground fell away as she was yanked upward. Some sort of netting made of thick leather strips folded tightly around her, making it impossible for her to move. She hung there for a second, stunned, then realized that someone was below her. When she angled her head downward, Buffy saw him.

A rough-looking man dressed in dark hunter's garb and boots stared up at her. Buffy couldn't decide which was more disturbing: the row of sharp teeth dangling from a cord around his neck, or the barrel of the long, oily rifle aimed at her head as she struggled vainly to free herself.

He grinned darkly, focusing behind the rifle's sight.

"Gotcha!"

CHAPTER 2

"Giles! GILES!"

"What the—" The hunter stopped and lowered the rifle slightly. He peered up at her, then experimentally thrust the tip of the barrel through the netting.

"Ow!" Buffy cried. Frustrated, she thrashed but still couldn't free herself.

Branches crunched as Giles lurched into the clearing. "Hey!" he yelled when he saw the guy standing below Buffy. Instantly, the hunter swung the gun in Giles's direction. "Whoa, now!" Giles sputtered and threw up his hands.

"The hands are good right about there," the man said coldly.

"Who are you?" Giles demanded. "What are you doing?"

"The name's Gib Cain," the hunter replied without lowering his weapon. "I'm the one with the gun. Which means *I'm* the one who gets to do the interview."

Buffy cleared her throat loudly. "Hey," she called

down, "before we get all chummy here, could we do something about this me being in a net thing?"

Cain glanced up at her, then lowered the rifle and pulled a knife from his belt. With three hard strokes, he sliced through the rope that held the net suspended above them. Buffy fell to the ground with an "Oof!"

Giles hurried to help free her. "You all right?"

"I could have done without the poking," she said, giving Cain a hard look.

Cain considered Buffy, then turned to Giles. "I got to say, I'm impressed."

"Excuse me?" Giles asked.

The hunter eyed Buffy again. "It's good to get the fruit while it's fresh."

Giles glared at him. "You'd be wise to take that back."

Cain shrugged, but his eyes were hooded. "Hey, what a man and a girl are doing in Lovers' Lane at night is nobody's—"

Giles started to move toward him, but Buffy stepped in between the two men. "It's not what you think, repulsive brain." It was obvious Cain wasn't convinced, so Buffy decided to go for the shock factor. "We're . . . hunting werewolves."

There was a beat of silence, then Cain broke into harsh laughter. "Sure," Buffy said in exasperation. "It's funny if you don't believe in werewolves—"

"No," Cain broke in. "It's funny thinking about you two catching one!" He shot Giles a humorous look. "This guy looks like he's auditioning to be a librarian. And you . . ." He shrugged and Buffy had the distinct impression he wanted to laugh all over again. "Well, you're a *girl*."

"I assure you," Giles said evenly, "she's quite capable."

"Uh-huh." Clearly Cain didn't believe him. "Let me

ask you something, sweetheart. Exactly how many of these animals have you taken out?"

Buffy hesitated. "As of . . . today?"

Cain fingered the necklace of sharp, pearly teeth around his neck. "I tore a tooth from the mouth of every werewolf that I killed. This next one will bring the total to an even dozen."

Not believing what she'd heard, Buffy looked at Giles, then back at Cain. "You're just going to *kill* it?"

"Well, see, that's the thing." Cain folded his arms around his hunting rifle. "Their pelts fetch a pretty penny in Sri Lanka, and it's a little hard to skin 'em when they're alive."

Giles's mouth fell open. "You hunt werewolves for sport!"

Cain wasn't at all vexed. "Oh, no. I'm in it purely for the money."

"And it doesn't bother you that a werewolf is a person twenty-eight days out of the month?" Buffy demanded.

For a second, Cain looked thoughtful. "You know, it does bother me. Quite a bit." Then his swarthy grin returned. "That's why I only hunt them the other three." He kept smiling as he began gathering the tangled net. "I'd really love to stay and chat, but I'm on a tight schedule. Any idea where else the boys and girls like to get together around here?"

Buffy couldn't follow. "You're looking for a party?"

"No," Cain told her, "but the werewolf is. They're suckers for that whole 'sexual heat' thing. Sense it miles away. But since little doggie ain't here, I guess he found another place."

The wheels clicked in Buffy's brain. "Sorry. Wish I could help you."

"But you don't know squat?" Cain shouldered the rest of his gear. "Gee, what a surprise."

Buffy and Giles watched him stomp off, then she

snatched her bag of supplies out of Giles's hand and headed in the opposite direction.

"Where are we going?" Giles asked as he kept up with her.

"I think I know where to look," Buffy said with determination. "We just have to make it there before *Mein Furrier.*"

The night was cool and way too dark for Theresa's liking. She clutched her jacket closer, feeling the weight of the book bag on her back, and stepped up her pace. All she wanted was to get home, and when she heard a rustling in the bushes somewhere behind her, she wished she'd paid more attention in Ms. Litto's class.

She stopped and looked back, trying to appear brave even though she wasn't very. Nothing, at least as far as she could tell. She started walking again, a little faster this time. In only a few more seconds, she heard the rustling sound repeat, and this time it was followed by a growl. The earlier reports of animal attacks filled her head and she looked behind her again, then gave in to the urge to run.

She wasn't very graceful or quick about it, and while Theresa knew she ought to keep her eyes straight ahead, she couldn't resist the urge to twist around yet again to see if she was being followed. But this time when she turned back to watch where she was going, she ran full tilt into another person.

Theresa bounced off the guy's chest with a little scream. She managed not to scream again only because he didn't grab for her.

"Everything okay?"

Her breath was ragged and it took a second or two, with her looking anxiously over her shoulder, to find enough air to talk. "I just—I thought I heard something," Theresa finally managed. "Behind me."

The guy in front of her frowned and stepped to the side of her, carefully scoping out the empty street. Nothing moved. "No one there."

Embarrassed, Theresa peered down the sidewalk once more. "Oh . . . I guess I was wrong. I could have sworn—"

"It's okay," he said reassuringly. He was tall and good-looking, dressed smartly in leather pants and a black overcoat. His words were calm and not at all condescending. "It can get pretty scary out here, all alone at night."

"Yeah," Theresa agreed nervously.

Her rescuer's expression brightened. "Hey," he said, "don't I know you from somewhere? Don't you go to school with Buffy?"

Relief flooded Theresa. "You know Buffy?" Buffy Summers had this way about her, an odd ability to stop bad things from happening, even if no one ever talked about it. If this guy knew her, he had to be okay and she would be safe with him. Theresa was certain of it.

"I do," he told her. "Very well." He touched her elbow and steered her forward until she was walking next to him. "Come on," he said, giving her a sweet smile and checking behind them one more time. "I'll get you home."

The Bronze was smoking tonight. A good band, a more than ample crowd, lots of touchy-feely going on with the couples around her.

And here sit I, Willow thought. *With my "date."*

From her spot on the couch next to Willow, Cordelia frowned. "I mean, with Xander it's always 'Buffy did this' or 'Willow said that.' Buffy, Buffy, Willow, Willow. It's like I don't even exist."

Willow nodded, inwardly marveling that she could so totally sync with what Cordelia was thinking. Surely this would put a bad spin on the universe. "I sometimes feel like that."

"And then," Cordelia continued, "when I call him on it, he acts all confused, like I'm the one with the problem."

"His 'Do I smell something?' look," Willow said knowingly.

Cordy nodded. "All part of his little guy-games. It's like he's there, but then he's not there. He wants it, but then he doesn't want it."

Too true, Willow thought. Aloud, she said, "He's so busy looking around at everything he doesn't have that he doesn't even realize what he *does* have."

Her seatmate gave her an arched look. "But he should at least realize that *you* have Oz."

A part of Willow was rather horrified that she was in a semi-bonding conversation with, of all people, Cordelia. Another part of her desperately felt the urge to talk. "I'm not sure I do," she finally said. "Oz and I are in some sort of holding pattern. Only without the holding." She paused. "Or anything else."

Cordelia frowned. "What's he waiting for? What's his problem?" She looked disgusted. "Oh—that's right. He's a guy."

"Yeah," Willow agreed. "Him and Xander. *Guys.*"

Cordy sat back in a huff. "Who do they think they are?"

"A couple of guys," Willow answered sagely. They nodded in agreement—

And something huge and hairy fell from the ceiling and crashed onto their table.

Werewolf!

Screams erupted as teenagers fled in all directions. Willow and Cordelia screamed along with everyone else and threw themselves backward as the creature swiped at them and missed. They scrambled from their seats and Willow got a grip on Cordelia's arm, pulling her along. "Come on!" she shrieked. "This way!"

Somehow they made it outside despite the crush for the door and the tables and chairs that went flying around them. Cordelia was right on her heels as Willow pounded out of the Bronze, shouting mental thanks as she saw Giles's car pull up.

"Looks as though your hunch was right," she heard Giles say to Buffy.

Her pal threw open the passenger door. "How could a werewolf resist Sunnydale's own House o' Hormones?"

"The werewolf!" Willow cried as she ran up to the car. "It's in there!"

From behind her, she heard Cordelia's voice reach a new level of strident as she ranted at the doorman. "You could be a little more discriminating with that velvet rope!"

Willow pulled on Buffy's sleeve. "It went upstairs!"

Buffy nodded and dashed for the entrance. Willow watched her disappear inside the Bronze just as a final, panicked couple lurched out. Then they were in the clear, and she had to bite her lip when someone reached out and slammed the door shut behind her best friend.

Now it was just Buffy, and the werewolf.

Great, Buffy thought. *Why do I always end up alone in dark places with creepy monsters?*

Oh, that's right. It's that 'Slayer' thing again.

So be it.

She crept forward, studying the shadows cast amid the broken chairs and overturned tables. Up the stairs and into more darkness. *Nice doggie, heel. But where did it go?*

She caught a movement from the corner of her eye and angled toward it, only to discover her own reflection in a mirror. She paused for a second, frowning at herself, then realized what was wrong about it—

The werewolf was right behind her.

Buffy spun out of its way as it leaped, barely avoiding the wicked slash of its claws. Crazy thoughts of a Slayer with werewolf blood—how would Giles control *that?*— ran through her head as she dodged and kicked, fighting to stay out of its range. It crashed backward, snarling viciously, and she grabbed at the chance to unshoulder her bag and yank out a length of heavy, iron chain. When it came at her again, she swung the chain for all she was worth; her reward was seeing it wrap solidly around the beast's neck.

The werewolf's paws came up and grasped it, the humanity deep within its form giving its fingers flexibility where there should have been none. Buffy held on tight and for her effort got thrown across the room when the creature whirled in an attempt to get free. With her hold lost, she heaved herself back to her feet in time to see the werewolf pull the chain loose. Instead of attacking again, it ran in the other direction and dove straight through the second floor window—

—and disappeared into the night.

"You let it get away," Gib Cain said. He seemed not at all surprised.

"I didn't *let* it do anything," Buffy said hotly. "I had the chain around its neck."

"Chain?" Cain rolled his eyes. "What were you going to do, take it for a walk?"

"I was trying to lock it up," she said as she folded the length of metal back into her bag.

"That's beautiful," Cain said, shaking his head. The interior of the Bronze was a wreck and he glanced at the destruction. "This is what happens when a woman tries to do a man's job."

"Now you look here, Mr. Cain," Giles said stiffly, "this girl risked her life trying to capture a beast that you haven't as yet been able to find."

"Uh-huh. And Daddy's doing a great job carrying her bag of Milk Bones." He smirked at Giles's outraged expression, then leaned in until he was right in Buffy's face. "You know, sis, if that thing out there harms anyone, it's going to be on your pretty little head."

Buffy just glared at him, and after a moment, he turned on his heel and headed for the door. Right before he left, he gave one parting shot. "I hope you can live with that."

She didn't drop her gaze. "I live with that every day."

Disgusted, Cain shook his head again as he walked away. "First they tell me I can't hunt an elephant for its ivory. Now I've got to deal with People for the Ethical Treatment of Werewolves."

Buffy stood and stared after him, then felt Giles take the bag and zip it closed. He touched her elbow to pull her attention away from the hunter. "Let's move out."

Ah, the sweet, dark night. So filled with life, and unlife, with potential.

Like that creature up ahead, sniffing like an obedient little mutt at the trail of blood Angel had left on the sidewalk.

Amused, Angel watched it from a half a block away. Darned good sized werewolf, plenty of teeth and muscle. When the sun rose and chased away the moon, who was it? It didn't matter; there really wasn't room in Sunnydale for another type of night hunter. And he knew just the thing that would get Buffy hot and heavy on the notion of eliminating this one.

Five yards, four, three—

Angel let Theresa's body *thump* to the sidewalk in front of the beast.

Five feet away, the werewolf froze and its eyes locked with Angel's. They studied each other and Angel mimicked its movement as it tilted its head first one way, then another, as though trying to understand what it was seeing—prey, but not prey. To drive the point home, Angel hissed at it, showing his full, bloodied teeth. Put on the defensive, the beast snarled in response and swiped at him. Safely out of range, Angel only grinned, then backed away and drifted out of sight as the werewolf leaned curiously over Theresa's corpse.

A second or two later, Angel's sharp smile widened as he heard the hairy beast howl mournfully at the moon.

The Point again, and wasn't it a sting that she seemed to always be on the *out*side of things here? But it was nearly dawn and Buffy sighed as she made her way back to Giles's car. She could hear the sound of a newscast on the tinny radio all the way across the now-empty parking lot—

"*. . . the negotiations were tabled when West-leader Petrie could not come to terms with the leader from the East. Petrie said a strike is inevitable.*"

—but when she got within range, the car was empty.

"Giles?" Panic filled her and she darted to the window. *What if the werewolf had found him and dragged him away? What if he was dead?* She yanked open the door, half yelling—

"Blaerg!" Giles cried and sat up on the front seat.

Buffy exhaled in relief and climbed inside the auto. "Oh—I didn't see you there. I thought something had happened."

"No, no," Giles managed. His hair was mussed and

his voice was groggy with sleep. "I was just . . . I'm okay." He blinked. "Fine. Uh—any sign of the were-wolf?"

"No." She gave him a sidelong glance. "I'm guessing you didn't see anything, either. From that vantage point of having your eyes closed."

Giles looked guiltily at his watch, then gazed out the window. "Sorry. It's going to be light soon. I suppose we should be heading—"

"Wait!" Buffy interrupted. She leaned forward and twisted the volume knob on the radio.

"—police say that the incident was apparently connected to the animal mutilation which occurred the night before last. The coroner's office has iden-tified the body as that of Sunnydale High School student Theresa Klusmeyer, age seventeen. The au-thorities ask that anyone with further informa-tion—"

Giles reached over and turned off the radio as Buffy slumped on the seat, devastated. *Theresa, dead?* But how could that be when it seemed like gym class had only been a couple of hours ago?

"Buffy," Giles said gently, "we're going to get this thing. We have another whole night." When Buffy didn't answer, he continued. "There's nothing more we can do now—it *is* sunrise. That werewolf isn't going to be a werewolf much longer."

No, Buffy thought, *it isn't.*

And Theresa isn't alive anymore either.

CHAPTER 3

He could feel the sun, and it was warm and bright. There was a breeze ruffling around him that brought the sound of birdsong to his ears, and it took a moment for him to realize that something else was sort of . . . *growling* along with it. He scrunched his eyes shut against the brightness and stretched, feeling and hearing his joints pop loudly. He felt a vague, not altogether unpleasant ache that made him groan, and *that* sound grew out of the previous weird growl.

He opened his eyes and saw a leafy canopy of sun-splashed green overhead.

Wrong.

Where was his bedroom ceiling?

Struggling upright, he stared at the woods surrounding him—vaguely familiar, perhaps the ones behind his own house. Like most forested areas, it had trees and grass and rocks, and probably a thousand small creatures and insects. It was *not* supposed to have, as he then discovered, his own buck-naked body lying behind a rock.

About the only thing Oz could think of to say out loud was a single, bewildered, "Huh."

Home. It should have surrounded him like an old friend, drawn him in and comforted him. Home was where you ran when you got your knee scraped or your ankle twisted, or you found out the girl you had a crush on liked the boy down the street better.

Or when you woke up in the woods without your clothes.

Oz picked up the phone and dialed his aunt's number from memory. The anticipation of hearing her voice, and of what he had to ask, made him shaky. A moment later, she answered the phone.

"Aunt Maureen? Hey, it's me—what? Oh, actually, it's healing okay." He held up the finger with the small bandage on it and studied it. So small, but so much possibility in there. "That's pretty much the reason I called. I wanted to ask you something."

Oz paused and silence filled the telephone line. His aunt didn't say anything and there was probably a whole two seconds of lag time between his words. It felt like a lifetime.

"Is Jordy a werewolf?"

He heard Aunt Maureen answer and felt it sink in at the same time he heard himself keep going with the conversation. He was pretty proud of himself.

"Uh-huh. And how long has that been going on? Uh-huh." *Wait*—she'd asked him something— *Never mind;* he really didn't feel up to sharing.

"What—no. No reason," Oz said in response. "Okay, well, thanks. Love to Uncle Ken."

She said good-bye—at least he thought she did—and

he hung up. Then he sat there for a while, taking in her answer and just staring at nothing.

Home.

It brought no comfort this time.

"I can't believe I let that thing get away," Buffy said. "Cain was right. I should have killed it when I had the chance!"

Willow looked up to see Oz coming in the door to the library, and despite the circumstances, she couldn't help smiling.

"Killed what?" he asked. He looked a little dazed.

"The werewolf," Giles said tiredly. "It was out last night."

Two steps brought Oz over to Willow. "Is everyone okay?" he asked anxiously. "Did anybody get bitten? Or scratched?"

His concern was touching. "No," Willow assured him. "We're fine."

"Gladness," he said, obviously relieved.

"Yeah, but he got someone," Buffy put in. "Theresa."

Oz's eyes widened. " 'Got' as in . . ." At their expressions, his voice trailed off and he leaned against the wall. "Oh . . . I'm sorry."

"And," Buffy continued, "I could have stopped it."

Giles rubbed his chin. "Well, we have one more night."

Oz frowned. "Another night?"

"Oh, yeah." Buffy's jaw was rigid. "Believe me, I'm going to give that wolfie something to howl about."

"Huh," Oz said.

Xander unfolded himself from the chair on the other side of the table. "But while we hang here doing nothing, there's a human werewolf walking around out there, probably making fun of us."

"The way werewolves always do," Willow said dryly.

111

She shot Oz a humorous look but he didn't seem to notice. Instead, he had a question of his own.

"But there's really no way to tell who it is?"

"Sure there is," Xander said confidently. "Giles knows stuff. And I'm practically an expert on this subject."

A corner of Willow's mouth lifted. "On account of how you were once a hyena."

Oz blinked. "Xander was . . . ?"

"Before we knew you," Willow told him.

Xander paced around the table, finally stopping in front of Oz. "I know what it's like to crave the taste of freshly killed meat. To be taken over by those uncontrollable urges—"

"You said you didn't remember anything about that," Buffy interrupted.

Derailed, Xander looked sheepish. "I said I didn't remember anything about that . . ." He cleared his throat. "Look, the point is, I have an affinity with this thing. I can get inside of its head." He closed his eyes and swayed for a few moments, then began to mumble to himself. "I'm a big, bad wolf." Eyes closed, Xander had no idea of the look that Willow exchanged with Buffy. "I'm on the prowl. I'm sniffing, I'm snarling, I'm a slobbering predator. I'm—"

He stopped, staring at Oz. "Wait a second. It's right in front of us. It's *obvious* who I am!"

Willow, Oz and the rest of them tensed.

"I'm Larry!"

When they all stared at him blankly, Xander began to tick off points on his fingers. "The guy's practically got 'wolf-boy' stamped on his forehead. You got the dog bite, you got the aggression. Not to mention the excessive back hair."

Buffy looked thoughtful. "He was awfully gleeful about tormenting Theresa."

Willow Rosenberg

Willow: "We're just friends. We used to go out, but we broke up."
Buffy: "How come?"
Willow: "He stole my Barbie. We were five."

Xander: "It's life on the Hellmouth."
Buffy: "Let's face it. None of us is ever going to have a normal, happy relationship."

"The one boy that's really liked me and he's a demon robot. What does that say about me?"

"He's great. We have a lot of fun. But I want some smoochies."

—Willow

Willow: "So I'd still if you'd still."
Oz: "I'd still. I'd very still."
Willow: "Okay. No biting, though."

"I mean, I'm not like a full-fledged witch—that takes years.
I just did a couple of pagan blessings and teeny glamour
to hide a zit."

—Willow

Oz looked at them. "Still, that doesn't necessarily mean that—"

"I'm going to go talk to him," Xander announced as he strode to the door. "Force a confession out of him!"

"Good," Giles said, unconvinced. "Good. In the meantime, we need to cover our bases. Willow, check the student files. See if anyone else fits the profile." He headed for his office, motioning for Buffy to follow. "Buffy?"

"Where are we going?" she asked.

"If none of that works," he told her, "I think I may have an alternative."

"Yeah. Me and the werewolf, alone in a cage for three minutes," Buffy said sharply. "That's all I ask."

Willow watched them go, then turned to Oz, who was staring numbly after them. Now it was just her and him. When he just kept staring into space, she finally broke the silence. "Are you okay?"

"What?"

"You kind of knew Theresa," she said hesitantly.

Oz turned toward her, but Willow still wasn't sure he was really *there*. "Oh, yeah. I'm trying not to think about it. It's . . . a lot."

"It is." She nodded for emphasis. "But we can do stuff to help. Sometimes it feels good to help."

"Uh-huh."

"Like looking up stuff?" Willow suggested bravely. "I'm going to be doing that most of the night. You could help me . . . help together—"

"I can't," he said before she could finish. "I'm . . . busy."

"Oh." She hadn't quite been prepared for that. "So—"

"I . . . I gotta go."

Willow didn't even have a chance to say good-bye before he turned and walked out. She could only sit there and watch him go, and wonder what just happened.

She didn't see Buffy standing at the door to Giles's office and watching with her, and silently sharing her pain.

Xander could hear the faucet running and knew that Larry was the only one in the locker room—he'd shadowed him for the last twenty minutes until Larry'd stopped in here. When the jock rounded the corner, Xander was right in his face.

"Harris!" Larry exclaimed as he jerked to a stop. "Geez—next time wear a bell!"

Xander didn't move out of his way. "Why so jumpy, Larry?"

"Geeks make me nervous," Larry said without missing a beat.

"Is that really it?" A corner of Xander's mouth turned up. "Or is there something you're hiding?"

Larry leaned toward him. "I could hide my fist in your face." He stepped around Xander and opened his locker; plastered to every inch inside the door were pictures of bikini-clad girls and models.

Before Larry could reach for his books, Xander slammed the door shut again. "I know your secret, big guy. I know what you've been doing at night."

Larry turned slowly toward him. "You know, Harris, that nosy little nose of yours is going to get you into trouble someday." Suddenly his ham-sized fist snagged Xander's collar and he yanked him nearly off his feet, then slammed him against a locker. "Like *today*."

But Xander didn't bat an eye. "Hurting me isn't going to make this go away. People are still going to find out."

Larry let him go with a little shove, then exhaled. "All right, what do you want? Hush money—is that what you're after?"

"I don't *want* anything," Xander told him. "I just want to help."

The other teen shot him a disgusted look. "What—you think you have a cure?"

Xander shook his head. "No, it's just . . . I know what you're going through because I've *been* there. That's why I know you should talk about it."

Larry gave a little laugh. "Yeah, that's easy for you to say! I mean, you're a nobody, but I've got a reputation."

"Larry, please—before someone else gets hurt." Xander waited.

The bigger teenager slammed a fist against his locker, then stared at the floor. "If this gets out, it's *over* for me. Forget about playing football—they'll run me out of this town. I mean, come on. How are people going to look at me after they find out I'm gay?"

Xander froze, but Larry didn't notice. "Wow," he said. He looked at Xander in awe. "I *said* it! And it felt . . . okay. I'm gay." He raised his voice. "I am *gay!*"

Xander found a painful smile. "Heard you the first time."

Larry spun happily. "I can't *believe* it—it was almost easy. I . . . I never felt like I could tell anyone. And then you, of all people, bring it out of me!"

Xander swallowed hard. "It . . . probably would have slipped out even if I wasn't here."

"No." Larry shook his head emphatically. "No, because knowing you went through the same thing made it easier for me to admit."

Xander's mouth dropped open. "The same thing?"

"It's ironic," Larry said. His face was sincere. "I mean, all those times I beat the crap out of you, it must have been because I recognized something in you that I didn't want to believe about myself."

"Larry, no," Xander said in desperation. "I am not—"

Larry clapped him on the shoulder companionably. "Of course, of course. Don't worry—I wouldn't do that to you." He leaned close and gave Xander a buddy-buddy smile. "Your secret's safe with me."

And left Xander staring after him in dismay.

"So, what's the scuttlebutt?" Buffy asked from behind her. "Anybody besides Larry fit our werewolf profile?"

Willow looked up and hid a smile as her friend perched on the edge of the desk. "There is one name that keeps getting spit out. Aggressive behavior, run-ins with authorities, about a screenful of violent incidents—"

Buffy broke in when she focused on the information displayed on the screen. "Okay, most of those were not my fault. Somebody else started them—I was just standing up for myself."

"They say it's a good idea to count to ten when you're angry," Willow said calmly.

Buffy glared at her. "One, two, three—"

Willow grinned. "I'll keep looking."

Buffy's voice softened. "I noticed you're looking solo."

"Yeah. Oz wanted to be somewhere that was away." She stared at the keyboard for a moment, losing her train of thought. "From me."

"I'm sorry."

Willow shrugged. "I can't figure him out. He's so hot and cold. Or . . . lukewarm and cold."

Buffy nodded sympathetically. "Welcome to the mystery that is men. I think it goes something like they grow body hair, they lose all ability to tell you what they really want."

Willow frowned. "That doesn't sound like a good trade." Outside the library, they heard the muffled sound of the bell ringing for class. She turned off the computer and followed Buffy to the door.

Buffy gave her a sidelong glance. "Well," she said, "you want to up the speed quotient with Oz, maybe you need to do something daring. Maybe you need to make the first move."

Willow chewed her lip nervously. "That won't make me a slut?"

Buffy's smile said it all as they entered the noisy hallway. "I think your reputation will remain intact."

"It used to be so easy to tell if a boy liked you," Willow mused as they walked. "He'd punch you on the arm, and then run back to his friends."

"Those were the days."

"Hey," Xander exclaimed from behind them with a punch to Buffy's arm.

Willow turned away. "I'll see you guys later. Cordelia asked me to look over her history homework before class. I think that means I might have to do it."

Buffy and Xander watched Willow go. Xander's expression was vaguely troubled. "Wow. Those two gals have been hanging out a lot together." He and Buffy began heading down the hallway. "This would be a good time to panic," he muttered beneath his breath, but Buffy still caught the words and had to choke back a laugh.

Instead, she asked, "How'd it go with Larry?"

"What's that supposed to mean?" Xander demanded defensively.

Buffy peered at him as she reached her locker and opened it. "I think it's supposed to mean 'How'd it go with Larry?' "

"He's not the werewolf," Xander said quickly. His words were practically tumbling over themselves. "Can't we just leave it at that? Must you continue to push and push?"

"Sorry," Buffy said, taken aback. "I was just wondering—"

"Well he's not!"

"Okay."

"Okay," Xander repeated.

Weird, but then Xander was always a bit high on the oddity scale. Buffy shrugged it off. "But there goes our lead suspect," she said, slumping against the locker. "Which puts us right back at square boned."

Xander tried to look perky for her benefit. "You're not boned. You're Buffy, Eradicator of Evil. Defender of . . . things that need defending."

"Tell that to Theresa," Buffy replied. Awful, imaginary images filled her head. "She could have used some defending before she was ripped apart by that . . ."

"Werewolf," Xander offered when she didn't finish.

Buffy's eyes narrowed. "Nowhere in any of the reports did it say anything about her being mauled. They were linked to the animal attacks from the other night, so we just *assumed* werewolf."

Xander was clearly puzzled. "What else would we have assumed?"

Buffy hated Sunnydale Funeral Home. There were too many funeral homes and cemeteries in Sunnydale to begin with—for obvious reasons—and she felt she'd had to visit this one *way* too often. What she was looking at now didn't help matters.

Theresa's face was powdered to pale perfection, but when she used a forefinger to pull down the floral scarf around the dead girl's neck—

"Vampire."

"So that's good, right?" Xander asked. "I mean, in the sense that the werewolf didn't get her and—" He fumbled, then rubbed his eyes. "No. There is no good here."

"No good." Buffy stared sadly at Theresa. "Instead of not protecting Theresa from the werewolf, I was able to not protect her from something just as bad."

She turned away from the coffin and moved to the satin sign-in book. The stand that held it wobbled on three rather skinny legs as she scrawled her name. "She had a lot of friends," she said softly.

"Buffy, you can't blame yourself for every death that happens in Sunnydale." Xander came around and faced her from the other side of the easel as she scanned the list of people who'd visited. "If it weren't for you, people would be lined up five deep waiting to get themselves buried. Willow would be Robbie the Robot's love slave, I wouldn't even have a head, and—" He choked momentarily and Buffy looked up to see him gawking at something behind her. "Theresa's a *vampire!*"

Buffy whirled in time for Theresa's full body tackle. They rolled, hammering at one another. But Theresa, as inexperienced in unlife as she had been in life, was no match for the Slayer. In a matter of seconds Buffy had thrown the vampire-girl across the room, snapped off one of the easel legs, and was straddling her. It was time for the ugly version of Theresa to bite the dust.

Buffy's arm came up, but before she could thrust the piece of wood home, Theresa locked eyes with her.

"Angel sends his love," she sneered.

Buffy froze. Theresa saw her opportunity and slammed her hand against Buffy's, knocking the stake away. They wrestled and Theresa's little surprise slowed

Buffy's skills; now it was Theresa who had Buffy pinned to the floor. Buffy struggled to keep the dead girl's fangs away from her throat and—

—Theresa exploded into vamp dust.

Xander stood behind the falling cloud of sooty brown with one leg of the book-signing easel pointed downward. "Are you okay?"

Angel had done this . . .

Buffy hauled herself to her feet. Everything around her—her body, her world, *everything*—seemed suddenly shaky and unreliable. "This isn't happening," she murmured. Her guilt was so huge she couldn't meet Xander's eyes.

"Buffy . . ." Xander touched her on the shoulder and she folded herself into his arms, hungry for even a temporary sense of security.

"He's going to keep coming after me," she said against his shirt. "Until . . ."

"Don't let him get to you." Xander's arms tightened around her. "He's not the same guy you knew."

God, how true was *that?* And here she was, safe for a time, being held by someone she could trust. By—

Buffy tilted her head back and looked at him. "Xander?" The response she saw in his eyes was the last thing she needed. She broke away. "Thanks," she managed, and he smiled. She swiped at her hair, having no idea what the struggle with Theresa had done to it. "Well, I've got a lot to do tonight."

"Yeah," Xander said.

"I should probably go do it."

She could feel his gaze on her as she left, and her hearing, so attuned to the things most people missed, easily caught the words he whispered to himself.

"Oh, no. My life's not *too* complicated."

* * *

The woods in this part of Sunnydale were dark and lush, a perfect place in which to pull his van and refill his stock. Gib Cain had everything he needed inside: a small, extremely hot stove, a melting pot and a half dozen oblong molds . . .

And, of course, the silver.

He hummed along with a song on the tape player as he carefully poured the melted metal into an empty bullet mold, then set it aside to cool. He had enough rifles, bows, arrows, nets and traps to bring down a couple of elephants, so one relatively small werewolf really wasn't going to be a problem. He had his bullets, and all the beast needed was a little incentive.

Finished with the ammunition, he set those tools aside, then leaned over and opened the door to a small refrigerator. The platter Cain pulled out held several pounds of fresh, red meat.

Smiling, the hunter sliced off the thickest parts and tossed them into his backpack.

Just a little incentive.

CHAPTER 4

Sunnydale, Oz thought. *Always an adventure.*

He sat at the dining-room table and took a deep breath, then grasped the cardboard box in front of him and tilted it. A set of heavy steel manacles and chains fell out, complete with padlocks. Yes, there was a key, but he'd hidden it, figuring that once he was in werewolf-mode he wouldn't be smart or dexterous enough to find it and use it. After all, hadn't Giles said the beast was nothing but pure animalistic instinct?

With his hands and ankles shackled together, Oz felt pretty confident that all he'd be able to do was writhe around on the floor. Luckily the other occupants of the house were out of town and the rest of Sunnydale would be safe enough, at least from him. He squeezed his eyes shut, then snapped the first manacle around his left wrist. He reached for the padlock—

Bang bang bang!

Oz jumped as someone pounded on the front door. No, he wouldn't answer it—there wasn't time. He picked up the padlock—

Bang bang bang!

—and dropped it. The sound had something to it, an undertone that told him the person at the door might just try the knob. Had he locked it? He couldn't remember. His nerves jangled as he glanced at the clock, but Oz undid the manacle and went to the door. When he opened it, his eyes widened.

"Willow! What are you doing here—"

Willow pushed past Oz without an invitation, then whirled and started talking. She needed to get this out before she turned Kentucky Fried. "I had this whole thing worked out and I had written it down, but then it didn't make any sense when I was reading it back."

Oz swallowed and looked around the room. "Willow, this is *not* a very good time—"

"I mean," she rushed on, "what am I supposed to think? First you buy me popcorn, and then you're all glad I didn't get bit. And you put the tag in my shirt, but I guess none of that means anything because instead of looking up names with me, here you are all alone in your house doing nothing by yourself!"

"Willow," Oz held out his hand. "We'll talk about this tomorrow, I promise—"

"No, darn it, we will talk about this *now!*" She stood her ground as he tried to take her arm, ignoring the fact that she was feeling a little airless. "Buffy told me that sometimes what the girl makes has to be the first move and now that I'm saying this I'm starting to think that the written version sounded pretty good but you know what I mean!"

He took her by the arm and tried to steer her back to the front door. "I know," he said. His voice was calm but there was something odd about it. "I know, it's me. I'm going through some . . . changes."

Her breathlessness changed to a tinge of irritation and she pulled out of his grasp and stomped back toward the dining room, where he couldn't try to push her out again. "Well, welcome to the world!" she exclaimed. "Things happen. You don't think I'm going through a lot?"

"Not like me."

Her eyebrows lifted. "Oh, so now you're special," she said smartly as she stopped by the table. "You're a special boy—" Her words sputtered out as she stared at the tabletop. "With chains and . . . stuff." She turned back to him. "Why do you have chains and stuff?"

"Willow, please," he said. Was that a desperate tone in his voice? Before she could decide, he shocked her by doubling over and clutching his stomach. "Get *out* of here!"

Her jaw dropped as he staggered behind the couch, then suddenly fell to the floor. "Oz? What is it?" The only answer was a strangled moan, and Willow hurried to peer over the piece of furniture. "What's wrong?"

Oz—*her* Oz—snarled at her from behind the face of the werewolf.

The scream that rippled from her throat was full strength and instinctive.

Oz—*it*—lunged for her and Willow threw herself out of reach and ran blindly through the house, hearing the creature growl as it scrambled over the couch. It followed on her heels as she pulled things onto the floor behind her, trying to slow it down—a coatrack, a kitchen chair, the trash bin, a pile of books from the counter. She made it to the back door and hurtled through it, slamming it behind her with as much force as she could—

Not enough. An instant later the werewolf leapt through; she had, maybe, a lead of ten yards. The back fence blocked her path and Willow grabbed the top of it and tried unsuccessfully to hoist herself over. She slid back down and heard the beast growl from only a few feet away, and that was enough encouragement to make her try again. This time she lurched over, then ran, as hard as she could, for her life.

Bushes and trees flashed by, blurry black shadows in the moonlight. She veered into the park without thinking, zigzagging down the path and sailing over one of the benches like she was a school track star. She kept running, hearing the werewolf snarling and snapping from somewhere behind her. But the park was much too open—the beast could see her without even trying. In a split-second decision, Willow angled into the woods, dodging between the trees like a football player.

It did her no good. The werewolf crashed through the thicket behind her. She *had* to put distance between them, but when she looked over her shoulder to check where it was—

Crash!

Her foot hooked beneath a fallen log and she tumbled headfirst to the ground.

All Willow could do was sit there, too dazed to move, and watch as the werewolf filled her vision.

Everyone always says that a drowning person sees his life flash before his eyes. Willow didn't know if this were true, but she was certain her replay was going to start any moment. She was paralyzed and terrified as the Oz-in-werewolf-body crouched and prepared to spring.

Then it stopped, lifted its head, and sniffed the air.

It looked off to the right, then back at her as if unable to decide. After a moment, it raised its face to the moon and howled. Then, unbelievably, it loped away.

Willow wasn't about to wait around and consider how fortunate she was. She scrambled to her feet and made for the safety of the high school.

Buffy heard a clang from the library as she hurried through the door. Giles had dropped a steel case on the table, and as she came over he began pulling out pieces of a high-tech rifle. "Sorry, I'm late," she said. "Had to do some unscheduled slayage in the form of Theresa."

Her Watcher looked up from where he was assembling the weapon. "She's a vampire?"

"Was." Buffy was unable to disguise her hurt. "Angel sent her to me. A little token of his affection."

Giles took a step toward her. "Buffy, I'm sorry—"

She held up her hand. When she spoke, her words came through gritted teeth. "Not now, Giles. We'll all have ourselves a good cry after we bag us a werewolf."

He nodded and turned his attention back to his project. "All set," he said as he screwed the final piece, a scope, into place. "Let's go find this thing."

"One question," Buffy said as they started for the door. "How exactly *do* we find this thing?"

Giles began to answer, then they both jumped as Willow dashed into the library. "It's Oz!" she cried. "It's Oz!"

"What's Oz?" Buffy asked.

Willow was gasping for air. "The *werewolf!*"

"Are you certain?" Giles demanded, shocked.

"Can't you just *trust* me on this?" Willow looked about to burst into tears. "He . . . he said he was going through all these changes, and then he went through all these . . . *changes!*"

Buffy squared her shoulders. "Where is he now?"

Willow looked back at the door automatically. "In the woods."

"Willow, it'll be okay." Buffy squeezed her friend's arm. "We're going to take care of everything."

Giles lifted the rifle, then primed it. "Let's go."

Willow's eyes were huge as she saw the gun. "Go *where?* You're not going to kill Oz!" She looked ready to panic. "I mean, sure, he's a werewolf, but I bet he doesn't mean to be!"

"Don't worry, Will," Buffy assured her. "We're not going to hurt him."

Giles turned the rifle until they could see it was filled with tranquilizer darts. "I put enough phenobarbital in here to sink a small elephant. It should be enough for a large werewolf."

Gib Cain crouched in the woods, his rifle, loaded with silver bullets, at the ready. When he heard the werewolf's soulful howl, he smiled in the darkness. "There you are," he whispered as he began silently working his way toward the cry.

It didn't take long to find the creature—Cain had set the perfect trap and the beast had taken the bait immediately. When the hunter crept to the edge of the clearing where he'd arranged the pile of meat, he could see the werewolf on the other side, sniffing the beef-scented air and carefully checking out the moonlit area. When all seemed okay, the werewolf edged toward the free meal.

"That's it," Cain murmured to himself, too low for even the werewolf's sensitive hearing to catch. "Let me see you . . ."

Another foot, then two, and the werewolf looked

around a final time, lowered its head, and began to devour the meat.

"Come on, suppertime," Cain whispered. He stood without making a sound and aimed.

"Good doggie. *Now play dead.*"

He squeezed the trigger at the same time someone smacked the side of his rifle and sent his best shot far off into the night sky.

Buffy got a good crack in, but Gib Cain was an experienced hunter and didn't let go of his weapon. From the clearing, she heard the werewolf snarl but she was too busy struggling with Cain to think about it. The man's face was grim and angry as he tried to pull the gun free; still, her strength caught him off guard. With very little effort she yanked the weapon from his hands, spun it, and slammed the butt into his stomach. He went down—

—and she found herself facing the snarling werewolf. She thrust Cain's gun forward to block it and the beast grabbed on and lifted her into the air. The thing tried with everything it had to bite and Buffy had to concentrate on keeping its jaws out of range and its claws occupied. Finally, as it reared back to try again, she managed to bring the rifle up and then down, clubbing it solidly on its skull. She knew the whole time that Giles was trying to get a shot in with the tranquilizer gun and heard Willow exclaim "Careful!" She just hoped her Watcher didn't accidentally shoot her instead of the werewolf.

Buffy played a sort of whirl game with the creature, putting its back to Giles, but not for long enough before once again it was *her* back facing the tranq gun. "Darn it," Giles exclaimed as she caught a glimpse of him trying in vain to get a shot. Then, just when she thought she had it under control, she went sailing through the air.

When she came down, it was on top of Giles and Willow.

The threesome scrambled around, trying to untangle themselves. Willow got free first, and Buffy was still hauling herself up when she saw the werewolf lock eyes with her friend, then jump for her.

Without time to think about it, Willow snatched up the tranquilizer rifle, squeezed her eyes shut, and fired.

The Oz-wolf howled in pain and reeled backward, clutching its chest. Willow knelt there, staring, as it staggered once, then collapsed. "I shot Oz," she said in horror.

"You saved us," Giles said gently. He took the gun from her and helped her stand.

"No wonder this town is overrun with monsters," said Cain. He looked disheveled and furious as he tramped over to them. "No one here's man enough to *kill* 'em."

"I wouldn't be too sure of that."

The hunter turned his head to see Buffy a few feet away. In her hands was his rifle. "You know," she continued, "I've been sick of you since the moment before I met you. And I've been waiting for just the right opportunity to take you on. But then I realized, a big, strong man versus a girl like me?" She looked down at his weapon. Suddenly her knuckles went white with effort and the steel barrel slowly began to bend. "Wouldn't be a fair fight," she said softly. She tossed the now worthless piece of junk to the hunter. "How about you let the door hit you in the butt on the way out of town."

He glowered at her as though he wanted to say something, then thought better of it. Instead, he simply shook his head and stalked away. Buffy dismissed him and turned back to her friend. "Willow?"

Willow had gone to the unconscious werewolf and now knelt next to him, her arms tightly folded around herself. "Is he going to be okay?" she asked Giles in a small voice.

Giles nodded. "He'll be a little sore in the morning, but he'll be Oz."

Willow looked at them, unsure, but at last she managed a tiny smile.

EPILOGUE

As it so often did, it seemed odd to walk down the hall at school the next day as if nothing out of the ordinary had happened the night before.

"This is all so weird," Xander said, as if he'd known her thoughts. "I mean, how are we supposed to act when we see him?"

"It's got to be weird for him, too," Buffy replied. "Now that we know so much."

Xander stared straight ahead. "All I know is I'll never be able to look at him the same way again."

Buffy frowned slightly. "He's still a human being. Most of the time."

Xander stopped, clearly confused. "Who are we talking about?"

"Oz," Buffy said, pausing with him. "Who are *you* talking about?"

Xander blinked. "No one," he said, a little too quickly.

A few feet away they saw a couple of the guys who'd always hung around with Larry. As a nice-looking girl passed them, one of them reached out and knocked her books from her hands. They leered at her as she stooped to retrieve them, and suddenly Larry stepped between them and the girl. "Here, let me get those," he offered, scooping up the books and handing them back. She took them and Larry came over to Buffy and Xander, ignoring the puzzled glances and comments of his former Larryettes. "Hey, Xander," he said. "Look—about what you did? Man, I owe you."

Buffy glanced from one guy to the other. "What'd you do?"

"It's really nothing that we should be talking about." Xander's voice was oddly strained and he locked eyes with Larry. *"Ever."*

Larry nodded. "I know, I know. It's just, well . . ." He reached over and squeezed Xander's shoulder, making her friend wince. "Thanks." He walked away.

"That was weird," Buffy said.

"What?" Xander demanded. "It's not okay for one guy to like another guy just because he happened to be in the locker room when absolutely nothing happened and I thought I told you not to *push!* "

Whoa, Buffy thought. *Bundle of nerves, aren't we?* "All I meant was that he didn't try to look up my dress."

"Oh, yeah." Xander coughed nervously. "That's the weirdness."

"Weirdness abounds lately," Buffy said as they headed outside. "Maybe it's the moon. It does stuff to people."

"I've heard that," Xander agreed.

She followed his gaze across the yard to where Willow was headed the other way. "It's certainly going to put a strain on Willow and Oz's relationship."

"What relationship?" There was a semistrident tone to Xander's voice. "I mean, what life could they possibly have? You're talking obedience school, paper training. Oz is always in the back burying their things. And that kind of breed can turn on its owner!"

"I don't know," Buffy said quietly. She saw Oz sitting on a bench on the far side and watched Willow angle toward him. "I kind of see Oz as the loyal type."

"All I'm just saying," Xander insisted, "is that she's not safe with him. If it was up to me—"

"Xander?" Buffy interrupted firmly. The look on her face was enough to finally shut him up. "It's not *up* to you."

Willow watched Oz for a few moments, then dug deep and found the courage to go stand in front of him. "Hey," she said in a soft voice.

For a second he didn't answer, then "Hey."

There was an awkward pause. "Did you want to go first?" she asked.

Oz studied his hands, as if he couldn't quite believe the secret hiding in them. "I spoke to Giles," he finally said. "He said I'll be okay. I'll just have to lock myself up around the full moon." He smiled slightly. "Only he used more words than that. And a globe."

"I'm sorry about how all this ended up," Willow said with a shameful expression. "With me shooting you and all."

"That's okay." He glanced at her. "I'm sorry I almost ate you."

She shrugged. "That's okay." Willow took a deep breath. "I kind of thought you would have told me."

Now it was Oz's turn to look embarrassed. "I didn't

know what to say. It's not every day you find out you're a werewolf. That's fairly freaksome. May take a couple of days getting used to."

Willow couldn't argue with that. "Yeah. It's a complication."

He stood and began walking with her. "So . . . maybe it'd be best if I just sort of . . ."

"What?"

His eyes were sad. "You know, like stayed out of your way for a while."

Willow frowned and turned to face him. "I don't know. I'm kind of okay with you being *in* my way."

Oz tilted his head as if he hadn't heard her correctly. "You mean, you'd still . . .?"

Willow smiled. "Well, I like you. You're nice and you're funny and you don't smoke. And yeah, okay, *werewolf,* but that's not all the time. I mean, three days out of the month *I'm* not much fun to be around either."

When it came, Oz's smile was wide. "You are quite the human."

"So I'd still if you'd still."

"I'd still." Oz nodded for emphasis. "I'd very still."

"Okay." Willow thought for a second. "No biting, though."

"Agreed," Oz said.

Satisfied, Willow hugged her books and stepped past him. She could feel him watching her as she left—

—so she turned back, took three quick steps and, enjoying his puzzled expression, kissed him full on the mouth.

Willow left him standing there and smiling as she strolled off. She thought she heard Oz say something—

"A werewolf in love . . ."

—but the noise of the yard carried the words away.

DAILY JOURNAL ENTRY:

Buffy has been gone like the entire summer . . . and no one's heard a word from her—not even her Mom. We're all worried sick, and Giles doesn't seem like the same person. Xander, Cordelia and I have been patrolling at night, and, well, while I wouldn't admit it to anyone's face . . . we're not very good. We've dusted a few vampires, sure—but probably only because it's been three against one. A couple . . . okay, *more* than a couple, have gotten away.

You know what? I don't even like to think about what would happen if we had to face down with something *really* icky—maybe some of the demons and monsters and stuff that Buffy has beaten in the past? Luckily there hasn't been any of that sort of stuff. Compared to the past, it's been pretty quiet.

I've tried so hard to understand why she would run out on us like she did. Buffy's so not the cowardly type—she's a stand-up and face-it woman. It must have been like a volcano for her . . . heating up from the inside, building until it all erupted in one huge, hurtful explosion. You know that time when Amy's spell backfired and we all fell in love with Xander? It's kind of like a dream, but I still remember crying to Oz on the phone about how wounded I was. For Buffy to deal about Angel . . . that must have been so much worse. And then it just . . . went on and on and on. I can't forget how he was before he lost his soul, how *good*—even for a vampire. The thing that he turned into was unimaginable. I've never known someone who could be so totally *cruel*.

I wonder what Buffy's doing right now? I'll bet it's something cool—like saving someone! So many people here have been helped by her—it's like she was *made* for that, you know? Beyond being chosen as the Slayer, I mean. She can't *not* do it. Even that time she was so sick in the hospital—she was willing to let herself get even sicker to help the children who were being attacked by that creepy Der Kindestod. I'm Buffy's friend, darn it . . . and so I have to think she's alive and "kicking." I can't let myself do what I know her mother is . . . making up all sorts of horrible scenarios, only imagining the worst.

But the thing that really bugs me . . . I know Buffy went through a lot and that she was, well, drowning in hurt. And that she like left in a hurry, all caught up in what had happened to her, and so freaked by having to kill Angel. But since then, has she ever thought about us? About *me?* I mean, who am I going to talk to now—Cordelia? Please, that's not even funny. Sure, there's Oz and he's my boyfriend—wow!—but I can't share girl stuff with him, stuff from the heart *about* him. And I don't think Cordelia *has* a heart. As for Xander—well, he's completely wrapped up in Cordelia. My best friend is gone, and I wish so much that I . . . well, just had someone to *talk* to about all the stuff that's going on in my life.

If Buffy were here, I think Mrs. Summers would be okay again, and Giles could at least start trying to heal. Buffy could tell me what she's feeling . . . and she could listen to me. We'd roll our eyes at Xander and wince at Cordelia—and it could be like it always was.

Wouldn't that just be the best?

/Press Enter To Save File/

FILE:
DEAD MAN'S PARTY

Prologue

It felt strange to be home, in Sunnydale, in her own room.

Buffy unpacked her duffle bag and put away her clothes, tucking them into the same old drawers and spots in the closet where they'd always gone before. It was the same . . . but not. Changed by her absence somehow—*she* was changed. Now they would have to learn about each other all over again.

And it was time to start the process.

She picked up her coat, then went down the hall to her mom's room. She walked in as her mother was swinging a hammer at a nail she'd positioned on the wall.

"Mom," Buffy began.

Joyce Summers jumped and missed the mark. Her final blow with the hammer bounced into the wall, leaving a half-dollar sized hole in the wallpaper. "Oh, Buffy!"

Buffy winced. "Sorry."

Joyce smiled. "No, no. Don't worry about it." She looked at the floor for a moment. "I guess I just got used to all the quiet while you were gone—but it's no problem. Look—" she raised a mean-looking mask from the dresser and hung it on the nail. The hole conveniently disappeared. "Do you like it?"

Buffy thought the mask, a half-face thing with slashes for eyes and a line of ugly, sharp yellow teeth, was awful. Still, she tried to cover her reaction. "It's, um, really . . ." *No good.* "I think I'd go with the hole."

"It's Nigerian," Joyce said. "We got a very exciting shipment in at the gallery. I thought I'd hang a few pieces in here. It cheers up the room."

The mask glowered darkly from the wall. "It's angry at the room," Buffy said. "Mom, it wants the room to suffer."

Her mom gave her a look. "You have no appreciation of primitive art—" She broke off as she saw Buffy's coat and a shadow passed over her face. "You going out?"

Buffy swallowed. "If . . . if it's okay. I'd like to find Willow and Xander."

Joyce inhaled. "And . . . will you be slaying?"

Buffy tried a small smile. "Not unless they give me lip."

"Can I make you a sandwich or something before you go?" her mom asked with false brightness. "You must be starving."

"I was until that four-course snack you served me after dinner."

"Well, then," Joyce said, reaching for her purse on the dresser. "You know, why don't I drive you? I mean, they could be anywhere—"

"Mom," Buffy broke in, "if you don't want me to go, just say so."

Joyce stopped, as though she suddenly realized what

she was doing. "No. I want to put this whole thing behind us. Get back to normal." She bit her lip. "You go—have a good time."

"Okay." Buffy backed out of her mom's bedroom before this clumsy conversation could pick up again. Then, because she felt she should, she stuck her head back inside. "Thanks."

Joyce jumped and hit the wall again with the hammer.

Sunnydale at night.

Buffy had almost forgotten how quiet and peaceful it could be, how deceptive. Like now, as she strolled along the sidewalk, passing houses where she could see the glow of lamps and televisions behind the curtains. Nothing moved, not even a cat or—

Wrong.

Up ahead, a noise, like someone knocking over a garbage can down an alley. Could be a dog, but it might be something far, far worse. Instinct demanded Buffy check it out.

She turned noiselessly into the alley. There, on the other side of a garage, was a man. Tall and dark-headed, dressed totally in black, an outfit meant to blend him into the background. She crept closer, focusing on her target and almost ready to grab hold of the back of his jacket—

—then her foot came down on a soda can.

Crunch!

The guy whirled and his hand came up. Everything in Buffy's vision fixed on the object in his hand, the same weapon that was swooping down and headed right for the center of her chest:

A stake.

CHAPTER 1

Buffy caught the piece of wood on the downward swing, using a concentrated effort *not* to flip the person who held it. After all, if he was hunting vampires he had to be one of the good guys. It took her one fast second to recognize the face behind the stake.

Xander.

They stared at each other, his expression a mixture of fright and surprised happiness.

"Didn't anyone ever warn you about playing with pointy sticks?" she asked with a small smile. "It's all fun and games until someone loses an eye."

She held onto the stake, but Xander was still stuck in stundom. "You . . . shouldn't sneak up on people like that." He stood there for another beat, then shook his head in disbelief. "Geez, Buff." Then they were hugging and starting to laugh—

A vampire exploded through the rotting wood of the garage wall behind them.

It grabbed Xander but let go as it got a solid kick in the side from Buffy. Both of them advanced on the stunned vamp, stakes in hand; both of them stopped when they each realized the other was ready to handle it. "Oh," Buffy said. "Go ahead."

Xander bowed out. "No, you go—"

But he seemed so capable. "No," she insisted. "It's—"

A shrill electronic squawk cut her off, then a tinny voice erupted from what Buffy realized was a toylike walkie-talkie hooked to Xander's belt.

"Come in, Nighthawk. Everything okay?"

She looked at Xander dubiously. "Nighthawk?"

Embarrassed, Xander fumbled at the device on his belt just as the vampire used their distraction to leap for Buffy. She went down under its weight, straining to keep the thing's snapping teeth away from her neck. The sound of running footsteps filled her ears and suddenly the vamp was gone, yanked off of her by two more people—Cordelia and Willow. They hurled it against the wall and tried to hold the struggling thing in place.

"Hello?" Cordelia gasped. "This would be dust time!"

Stake raised, Oz dashed up with Xander, but the girls were no match for the strength of the vampire. It kicked Oz out of the way, then one hard lurch sent Willow rolling onto Oz and Xander while Cordelia reeled backward into Buffy.

"Oh!" Cordy said in surprise. "Hey, Buffy—"

Behind her the vampire's mouth opened wide. Buffy gave Cordelia a shove that sent her into the rapidly growing pile of friends on the ground, and hammered the stake home.

Another vampire, dusted.

Buffy turned to face her friends as they sprawled on

the ground at her feet and stared up at her. Finally she said the only thing she could think of.

"Hey, guys."

Willow waited with the others as Buffy approached the door to Giles's apartment and reached for the heavy door knocker. Buffy hesitated and looked back at them. "Are you sure it's not too late? Maybe we should come back tomorrow."

No one said anything, and Willow could see Buffy squirming beneath their gazes. When Buffy had first disappeared, Willow had seen Giles kind of . . . turn in on himself. He'd never told Willow about what had happened, but she knew he'd gone to see Mrs. Summers. Afterward, he was much worse—more quiet and sad, and Willow thought it was a good bet that Mrs. Summers had blamed him for Buffy's leaving. With that on top of Angel killing Ms. Calendar, then leaving the body for Giles to find, she knew he had to be carrying a world of hurt.

Buffy started to reach for the door knocker again, then stopped once more. "What if he's mad?"

Xander raised one eyebrow. "Mad? Just because you ran away and abandoned your post and your friends and your mother and made him lie awake every night worrying about you?" He gave the others a skeptical look. "Maybe we should wait out here."

Buffy frowned at him, took a big breath, and finally knocked three times. There was a nervous pause, then the door swung open. Giles stood there, and Willow saw a whole bunch of emotions play across his features. Relief won, but he still seemed unable to speak.

"Check it out," Xander threw in. "The Watcher's back on the clock. And just when you were thinking career change, maybe becoming a 'Looker' or a 'Seer'—"

"Thank you, Xander," Giles said quietly. Xander's yammering fizzled out and for another long moment, the librarian didn't say anything at all. He and Buffy stared at each other, until at last Giles's face softened and he motioned them all inside.

"Welcome home, Buffy."

Willow and the others sat comfortably on two couches in Giles's living room. Willow thought Buffy looked okay—whatever she'd been into over the summer hadn't seemed to change her much except she had a new streak of blond across the front of her bangs.

"I got in a few hours ago," Buffy told them, "but I went to see Mom first."

"Yes, of course," Giles said. "And how did you find her?"

Buffy's answer held a hint of humor. "Well, I pretty much remembered the address."

A corner of Giles's mouth lifted. "I mean, how are things between you?" He stopped and they heard the sound of the teakettle whistling in the kitchen. "Ah, excuse me."

The five of them continued to yak among themselves as Giles got up and went to turn off the hot water. Willow watched him go from the corner of her eye. What was he feeling right now? She could imagine him standing in the kitchen, trying to go through the routine of readying snacks for his unexpected visitors. If it were her—if she'd had a single moment alone since Buffy had popped back into their lives—she'd probably be standing in there, fighting back tears. But this was Giles, and he was an adult and a man. He was probably just relieved to see Buffy had made it back safely.

"Okay," Oz said, "you're not wanted for murder anymore."

Buffy grinned. "Good. That was such a drag."

"So where were you?" Xander asked eagerly. "Did you go to Belgium?"

Buffy looked at him as though he'd suddenly grown an extra head. "Why would I go to Belgium?"

Xander made his eyes go wide. "I think the relevant question is 'why wouldn't you?' Bel-gium!"

They all laughed. "What about you, Xander?" she asked. "What's up with you?"

"Oh, you know." He shrugged. "Same old, same old—"

"Right, then," Giles said from the doorway. "Tea's on."

Still silent, Willow studied him. He looked okay, but there was wear around the edges. The Watcher hid his feelings well.

Cordy leaned forward and snagged a cookie from the tray. "Okay, were you, like, living in a box or what?"

Willow glanced at Xander and saw his eyes light up with curiosity. All this time, Xander hadn't said anything, but she knew he thought about Buffy constantly—he always had. Cordelia . . . well, she was just Cordelia, Miss I'm-The-Center-Of-The-Universe. In her own limited way she liked Buffy, but her only dilemma with Buffy being gone had probably been that the patrolling interfered with the summer social life she'd had planned for her and Xander.

Funny, while they'd all done a great job of not sharing their personal feelings, they *had* talked about Mrs. Summers and what it must have been like for her. The Summers's house had probably never seemed so big or empty or spooky. Except for Giles, the rest of them had families to go home to, people who surrounded them with love and laughter. Giles had his books—not the same thing, of course, but she was guessing they'd carried him through hard times for years. He seemed to take great comfort in them, but what had Buffy's mom done to deal with this? Did she have friends they didn't know about? The gang had visited her a couple of times over the summer, but the last time had been about two weeks ago. It'd been so awkward that they hadn't gone back— they'd just run out of stuff to say.

Now Buffy hesitated. "It's . . . a long story."

Xander grabbed his own snack. "So skip the heart-warming stuff about kindly old people and saving the farm and get right to the dirt—"

"Perhaps Buffy could use a little time to adjust," Giles interrupted. "Before we grill her on her summer activities."

"What he said," Buffy put in, looking relieved.

"Fair enough." Xander sat back. "In fact, you can leave the slaying to us while you settle in. We got you covered."

"I noticed," Buffy said, folding her arms. "You guys seemed down with the slayage. All tricked out with your walkies and everything."

Cordelia frowned. "Yeah, but the outfits *suck*. This whole Rambo thing is so over. I'm thinking more sporty—like Hilfiger, maybe."

"Still," Willow put in enthusiastically, "we're getting good. I mean, we dust, like, nine out of ten."

"Six out of ten," Oz whispered in her ear.

"Six out of ten," Willow repeated, still enthusiastic.

"Whatever," Xander said. "We've been kicking a little undead booty."

Buffy nodded. "Well, thank you for the offer, but I think I just want to get back to my normal routine. You know, school, slaying, kid stuff." She glanced at Xander. "In fact, I'm jonesing for a little brainless fun. What are you doing tomorrow?"

Uh-oh, Willow thought as an awkward silence fell over the group. "Oh, I would," Xander finally said as he put a hand on Cordelia's arm. "But I'm kind of tied up."

Cordelia smiled slyly at him. "You wish."

Buffy turned to Willow. "What about you, Will?"

She blinked. "Tomorrow? I . . ."

"Oh, come on," Buffy prompted. "Friends don't let friends browse alone."

Willow glanced at Oz, hesitated, then shrugged. "Okay. I had some school work, but . . . I can change my plans."

Giles cleared his throat. "As for school, Buffy . . . you know you'll have to talk with Principal Snyder before—"

"On it," Buffy agreed. "Mom is making an appointment with His Ugliness."

"It may be tough going," Giles commented. "He's quite emphatic about a Buffy-free Sunnydale High."

"No problem," Buffy said, but Willow thought privately that her friend was covering up her worry. "I'm bringing The Intimidator. One look at 'Mom Face' and I know she can break him."

Willow just hoped she was right.

"Absolutely not. Under no circumstance."

The Intimidator's "Mom Face" faltered as she and Buffy sat across from Principal Snyder. Buffy, unhappy but not particularly surprised, felt sorry for her mom as the older woman's expression went to disbelief. "But . . . you can't keep her out of school!" Joyce Summers exclaimed. "You don't have the *right!*"

Snyder gave them a thin-lipped smile that showed all his little teeth. "I have not only the right but also a nearly physical sensation of pleasure at the thought of keeping her out of school. I'd describe myself as *tingly.*"

"Buffy was cleared of all those charges," Joyce said hotly.

Snyder happily tapped his fingertips together. "Yes, and while she may live up to the not-a-murderer requirement for enrollment, she *is* a troublemaker, destructive to school property and the occasional student, and her grade point average alone is enough to . . ." He smiled dreamily. "I'm sorry. Another tingle moment."

Buffy's mother looked at him incredulously. "I don't see how you can be so cavalier about a young girl's entire future!"

The principal leaned forward. "I'm quite sure that a girl with talents and abilities such as Buffy's will land on her feet." He looked positively gleeful. "In fact, I noticed on the way in this morning that Hot-Dog-On-A-Stick is hiring." His gaze cut to Buffy. "You'll look so cute in that hat."

Buffy picked up her bag and stood. "Let's go, Mom."

"This isn't over," Joyce told Snyder as she moved to follow her daughter. "If I have to, I'll go all the way to the Mayor."

Snyder just sat there, unaffected. "Wouldn't *that* be interesting."

Out in the hallway, Buffy saw Giles coming toward them. Obviously he'd been trying very hard not to look like he was waiting for the outcome. "Well, how did it go?"

"Have you ever noticed his teeth?" Joyce asked fiercely. "They're like tiny, little *rodent* teeth—"

"Oh, dear," Giles said.

"Horrible, gnashing little teeth. You just want to pull them out with pliers."

Giles blinked at her. "Perhaps there's some way he can be overruled," he said as they moved farther down the hallway.

Buffy watched them go, knew they were discussing her "situation." Suddenly the bell rang and students poured from the classrooms lining the main hallway, moving smoothly around her like she was a pebble in the middle of a river. She felt about as big, too, when no one noticed her or so much as said "hi."

If Snyder wouldn't let her back into Sunnydale High, what was she going to do?

"Don't worry about school, honey." Later, Joyce pulled the car over to the curb where Buffy was supposed to meet Willow. "If we can't get you back into Sunnydale, maybe we can swing private school."

Buffy was horrified. "You mean like with the jackets and kilts? You want me to get field-hockey knees?"

Her mom just smiled. "It's not *that* bad."

Buffy looked at her hopefully. "What about home schooling? You know, it's not just for scary religious people anymore."

"We'll work something out. Okay?"

Buffy nodded and her mother leaned over and kissed her on the cheek. "Tell Willow I said hi," she called as Buffy got out.

Buffy watched her drive away, then wandered around outside the Espresso Pump as she waited for Willow. Maybe they could do a little shopping when she got here, or just sit and talk. It'd been ages since she had someone to really talk to. She could tell her about Lily and what had happened at the homeless shelter—Willow would remember Lily from when she'd been Chanterelle and seeking immortality with Billy Fordham. There was so much to catch up on.

Or not.

Shocked, Buffy looked at her watch and realized she'd been hanging around the coffee shop and daydreaming for almost half an hour. Where was Willow? It wasn't like her to be late like this.

Discouraged, Buffy checked her watch again, then settled on one of the beat-up couches the shop had put outside on the patio. Willow had said she was originally supposed to do school stuff—maybe that's what had made her so late.

Buffy decided to give it a few more minutes.

It was a lonely walk home. The streets and houses were familiar but the sight of them did nothing to comfort Buffy. Even her own house didn't look very welcoming as she turned up the walkway. It became even less so when a strange woman hustled out the front door.

Buffy stopped as the woman, blond and about her mom's age, noticed her. She hurried forward, smiling and fluttering like an oversized butterfly. "Oh, my word!" she exclaimed. "You must be Buffy! Look at you." Her smile widened. "Aren't you a picture!"

Buffy tried valiantly to smile back. "Thank you."

"I'm Pat," the stranger said, grabbing Buffy's hand and shaking it excitedly. "From your mother's book club? I'm sure she mentioned me."

"Actually—" Buffy began.

"I sort of took it upon myself to look after her while you were, you know, off and away or what have you." Pat bounced her head back and forth as Buffy stared. "Between your 'situation' and reading *Deep End of the Ocean,* she was just a wreck. You can imagine."

There was that "situation" word again. And *Deep End of the Ocean?* She opened her mouth to say something, but Pat was already dashing toward the street.

"Anyway, I'm off," she called gaily. "We're making empanadas in my Spanish class tonight. You go be with your mother. You two need to re-bond."

Yipes, Buffy thought and made for the front door. *The world's gone a little weird—maybe I'm safer inside.* She couldn't help feeling irritated as she went into the kitchen and found her mother paging through a cookbook. "Pat wishes us quality time," she said dryly.

Joyce looked up. "Oh, I met her in—"

"Book club. Got it."

Joyce nodded. "Before I forget, Willow just called."

Buffy's face clouded. "Where was she?"

"She got held up," Joyce told her. "But she said she tried to call."

"Was there a message?"

"No." Her mom looked back at her cookbook momentarily, then lifted her chin. "But I had a thought. What if I invited Willow and Mr. Giles and everybody over for dinner tomorrow night? Don't you think that would be nice?" When Buffy hesitated, Joyce hurried on. "Since I sort of already did, I'm hoping for a 'yes.' "

Dinner with Mom and the friends. "It would be fun," she managed.

Joyce smiled. "Great. Do me a favor? Run down and get the company plates?"

"Mom. Willow and everybody aren't company plate people. They're normal plate people."

"We never have guests for dinner," Joyce said sternly, giving her the "Mom Face." "Indulge your mother."

Buffy turned to go, then stopped and looked back. "So how come that works on me, but not on other people?"

Joyce didn't look up from her cookbook. "It's genetic."

Genetic, Buffy thought as she tramped down to the basement. *Does that mean I'll have a 'Buffy Face' when I get older? Ugh.*

She positioned a stepstool in front of the storage shelves so she could reach the plates, but stopped halfway up the climb. There, tucked facedown on a middle shelf, was a familiar framed photo—her, Xander and Willow. They all looked so happy, but she felt like she was looking at a picture of someone else's life. Would they ever be the same?

Buffy sighed and slid the photo back where it'd come from, then stretched overhead to pull out the box of company plates. Before she could get her hands on it, she bumped something else she couldn't see and felt the object come loose.

She yelped and barely kept her balance when the dead cat fell past her and landed on the floor with an ugly *thump*.

CHAPTER 2

A small, shallow grave in the backyard. Somehow, Buffy never thought she'd be digging one there.

Joyce had put the sad-looking, formerly gray cat into a plastic garbage bag. Now she stepped forward and dropped it gingerly into the hole Buffy had made behind the flower bed. Buffy looked from the bag to her mother. "Next time, *I* get to pick the mother/daughter bonding activity."

They regarded the tiny grave for a moment, then Joyce spoke. "Do you want to say something?"

Buffy made a *ewww* face. "Like what? Thanks for stopping by and dying?"

Her mother shrugged. "How about . . . good-bye, stray cat, who lost its way. We hope you find it."

She stopped as her words sunk in—bad choice. Without saying anything else, Buffy picked up the shovel and began to fill in the grave.

* * *

Her second night at home, in her own bed, and Buffy felt no more welcome than the night before.

The partial moon cast a cold, blue light through the window while the tree outside rustled in the breeze and sent shadows dancing across the walls. Of all the places she'd reacquainted herself with over the past few days, her room felt the least familiar of all.

Wasn't there any warmth at all left in her life?

With her daughter finally at home, elsewhere in the house Joyce Summers slept soundly. She never saw the eyes in the dark wood of the Nigerian mask begin to glow a rich, deep red, throbbing with secret power.

Outside, as if responding to an unearthly command, the loosely packed soil of the cat's grave began to quiver and heave. After a few seconds, the smooth surface split outward, and the cat, its fur matted and caked with grime, ripped its way free.

It fled into the bushes with an otherworldly yowl.

The school and the outside courtyard were completely deserted, silent and ghostly despite the bright sunlight spilling down. Nothing moved and not a single bird flew through the trees as Buffy wandered across the schoolyard.

A shadow moved at her side. She turned her head and saw Angel walk up beside her.

"I thought they'd be here," she said sadly.

"They are," he said, despite their empty surroundings. "They're waiting for you."

She gazed at him. The sunshine looked strange against his skin, making it seem even more pale than usual. "Am I dreaming?"

Angel smiled slightly. "I'm probably the wrong person to ask. You'd better go."

But she hung back. "I'm afraid."
"You should be," he said matter-of-factly.
And Buffy's alarm clock shattered the illusion.

"I've been on the phone with the Superintendent of Schools," Joyce said as she poured herself a cup of coffee. "At least he seems more reasonable than that nasty little horrid bigoted rodent man."

Buffy tensed. "Mom—"

"Anyway, I'm going in to speak with him this afternoon. As for private schools," she pushed a small stack of papers toward Buffy. "Miss Porter's accepts late admissions. I wrote the information down for you."

Buffy's mouth fell open. "A *girls'* school? So now it's jackets, kilts and *no boys?* Care to throw in a little foot binding?"

Her mother's expression turned hard. "Buffy, you've made some bad choices. You just might have to live with some consequences."

Buffy stood there, frozen, unable to process this horrible news. After a moment, Joyce's face softened. "Nothing's settled yet," she amended. "I just wish you didn't have to be so secretive about things." She picked up the dishrag and wiped the counter nervously. "I mean, it's not your fault you have a special circumstance. They should make allowances for you."

Buffy sighed. "Mom, I'm a Slayer. It's not like I have to ride the little bus to school."

Joyce pressed her lips together and opened the back door. "Couldn't you tell just a few people, like Principal Snyder? And maybe the police?" She leaned over and reached for the newspaper. "I mean, I'd think they'd be happy to have a superhero—is that the right term? It's not offensive, is it—*Aaaahgh!*"

Her mother's words ended in a scream and she threw herself backward as the cat—the very same one they'd buried the day before—scrambled through the door with a screech and disappeared into the house.

Buffy opened the front door for Giles, who stepped inside holding a small animal cage. "Welcome to the Hellmouth Petting Zoo." She motioned for him to follow her upstairs to her mom's bedroom, to where they'd easily tracked the cat.

With admirable fearlessness, Giles reached under the bed and grabbed the cat by the scruff of its neck. It hissed and yowled as he pulled it out and, holding it as far away as he could, deposited it into the cage. "Oh, my God," he choked out. "What a *stench.*"

"You know, I wanted Forest Pine or the April Fresh, but Mom wanted Dead Cat," Buffy said, trying to lighten the mood.

Bomb out. Giles looked at Joyce, but Buffy's mother was clearly freaked by the cat's resurrection. "I'll get it back to the library," he said. "See if we can determine its exact origin."

Joyce nodded but said nothing as he turned to go. Buffy saw Giles's gaze cut to the ugly mask on the wall, and he made another valiant effort to draw Joyce out. "That's striking. Nigerian?"

Joyce nodded, obviously glad to have something more rooted in reality to discuss. "Yes. I have this wonderful dealer who specializes in ancient artifacts—"

Oh no—another gallery chat. Buffy desperately needed something to do *away* from the house. "You know," she said, jumping in. "I love art talk as much as the next very dull person, but we have work to do. Giles—research mode?"

She started for the door, then realized Giles hadn't

moved. "Shouldn't you stay with your mother, Buffy? You must have—"

"Please," Joyce interrupted. "It's fine. She can go with you."

"Actually, she can't." He looked pained at Buffy's stare. "You're not allowed on school property."

"Oh." Stung, Buffy tried to be glib. "This marks a first. I want to go to school, but the school doesn't want me."

"I'm sorry," the librarian said gently. "I'll call as soon as I know something."

"And we'll see you tonight," Joyce put in. "Dinner?"

Giles looked startled, as though he'd already forgotten. "Of course. Tonight, then."

Wow, Buffy thought as she and her mother watched him leave. *Mom wants me to go out, Willow stands me up, Xander doesn't want to hang, and the school won't take me.*

She felt even more of an outsider than ever.

The zombie cat paced within its cage, every so often circling and growling at the air. Thoroughly disgusted, Willow and Xander watched it warily while Oz and Cordelia leaned in a little closer to check it out.

"Looks dead," Oz said in his best calm-Oz voice. "Smells dead. But moving around. Interesting."

The creature hissed and Cordelia made a face and moved to the other end of the table. "Nice pet, Giles. Don't you like anything regular? Golf or *USA Today,* or anything?"

"We're trying to find how and why it rose from the grave," Giles said as he paged through a volume on reanimation. "It's not as if I'm going to take it home and offer it a saucer of warm milk."

"I like it," Oz said. "I think you should call it Patches."

Willow had to smile. Maybe it was time for her to change the subject. "Hey," she said, "what about Buffy's welcome home dinner tonight. I told her mom we'd help out." She glanced around. "Bring stuff."

"I'm the dip!" Cordelia chirped.

There was a beautiful moment of silence as everyone stared at her, then Xander smiled sheepishly. "You gotta admire the purity of it."

"What?" Cordy demanded. "Onion dip. Stirring. Not cooking. It's what I bring."

Oz sat back and folded his arms. "We should figure out what kind of deal this is. I mean, is it a gathering, a shindig, or a hootenanny?"

"What's the difference?" Cordelia asked.

"Well, a gathering is brie and mellow song stylings," Oz explained. "Shindig: dip—" he nodded at Cordelia. "Less mellow song stylings, perhaps a large amount of malt beverage. And a hootenanny . . ." He tilted his head. "Chock full of hoot and a little bit of nanny."

"I hate brie," Xander said.

"I know," Cordelia agreed. "It smells like Giles's cat."

Giles looked up from his book. "It's *not* my—"

"And what would we talk about at a 'gathering' anyway?" Xander suddenly demanded. " 'So, Buffy—did you run into any nice creeps on your travels? And by the by, thanks for ruining our lives for the past three months—' "

"Xander—" Willow cut in.

"You know what I mean." His voice was almost snappish. "She doesn't want to talk about it, we don't want to talk about it, so why don't we just shut up and dance."

She'd had no idea Xander was so angry about this— he'd hid it well over the summer. His resentment seemed to rival her own feelings, the ones she'd kept so carefully hidden. "Buffy did say she wanted to loosen up," Willow said out loud. "Have some kid time." She paused, then turned to Oz. "Aren't you guys rehearsing tonight? Why don't you play at the party?"

Oz brightened. "Yeah, I think I could supply some Dingo action."

Giles paused from his studies, his expression slightly alarmed. "I'm not sure that a . . . shindig—"

"Hootenanny," Oz corrected.

"Hootenanny," Giles repeated, "is really the order of the day. Maybe something a little more intimate. Buffy just got home—I'm sure she's still feeling disoriented."

"All the more reason to make her feel welcome," Willow said enthusiastically. She looked to her friends for support and found it in their faces. "And a big party says *Welcome, Buffy!*"

"Okay." Xander stood. "So one vote from the old guy for smelly cheese night, and how many votes for actual fun?"

Hands shot up around the table, more than one to a customer, as they all eyed Giles. "All right, all right," he said, surrendering. "Have it your way. I'm just glad to have her home." He flipped a page in his book, and never noticed the inked illustration that looked just like the Nigerian mask in Joyce Summers's bedroom. Giles looked back as the page folded over to the next and the sketch disappeared.

"Now things can get back to normal."

Night fell gently on Sunnydale, and darkness slipped into the crevices of the Summers household. While the family readied itself downstairs for company, in Joyce's bedroom the Nigerian mask once again throbbed with strange life. Its eye cavities pulsated with red power as it sent out another silent call to those things unseen.

In the center of the highway across town, emergency lights strobed over police cars and officers, paramedics, and tow truck workers. A coroner's aide stood as he finished making a chalk outline around the body of a man sprawled on the roadway. The man's head had been horribly smashed in the accident, and the ambulance had arrived too late to save him. Now all that remained was the clean-up and reports of the police officers.

The aide walked back to his car and packed up his things, thinking about the paperwork he would have to fill out to cover this mess.

Splayed on the concrete a couple of yards away, the bloodshot eyes of the dead man suddenly opened wide. Unnoticed, he struggled up and lurched into the underbrush at the side of the road.

CHAPTER 3

Buffy, dressed in a pink satin dress with a beaded top, set the table, carefully arranging the good silverware around the company plates as per her mom's instructions. Her heart gave a little jump when the doorbell rang, but she hurried to open it anyway. It might be tough at first, but these were her friends—

"Hey, there you are!" said Pat as Buffy answered the door. "Not thinking about any more flights of fancy, I hope?" Disappointed, Buffy tried valiantly to hold her smile as Pat hustled inside and chattered away, not giving her a chance to reply. "Joyce said there was room for one more, so I said 'forget facial night and let's party!' I bet you like empanadas." She pushed a Tupperware container into Buffy's hands.

Buffy didn't know what to say. Finally, she gave Pat a thin smile and asked, "Do you want to see my mom?"

"Please," Pat said kindly.

"Mom!" Buffy yelled, too late realizing she actually sounded desperate.

Joyce hurried down the stairs, pleased to see Pat. "Oh, Pat—good. Buffy, I hope you don't mind."

The doorbell chimed again, saving her from having to answer. Relieved, Buffy yanked open the door, then her eyes widened.

"Hey, Buffy," said Devon. He stood there, loaded down with musical equipment, while a couple of giggling band groupies hovered behind him.

"Uh . . . hey." Stunned, she stared at them, trying to fit him into the neat little evening she'd imagined.

He grinned as he pushed past. "So, where do you want the band to set up?"

"The . . . band?"

Willow stood against the wall, swaying in time to the song that Dingoes Ate My Baby were playing in Buffy's living room. There seemed to be a hundred teenagers in the two main rooms of the house, most of whom she didn't know. How had they found out about the party? She and the rest of the Slayerettes had told a few people, but if this was word of mouth, it was awesome.

"Hey!"

Willow turned and saw Buffy standing behind her. She'd barely heard her friend's greeting over the noise. "Hey!" she yelled back.

Buffy gestured at the kids crammed into every corner. "This is . . . large!"

Willow nodded. "You like?"

"Yeah—it's great," Buffy shouted back. "It's just—I was just sort of hoping it would be us."

Willow shook her head, catching only a few of Buffy's words. "Sorry—what?"

Buffy tried again. "This is amazing. But I was sort of hoping it would be a gathering of the gang—"

Willow smiled and shook her head again. She mouthed the words "I can't hear you!" and looked back at the band, giving up.

But Buffy wasn't ready for that yet, and Willow felt her friend pull her out of the living room and a little way down the hall, where they could actually hear each other talk.

"Is everything okay?" Buffy asked her. "You seem to be . . . avoiding me. In the one-on-one sense."

Willow tried her best to smile, hoping Buffy couldn't see how uncomfortable she was. *Had* she been avoiding her best friend? Maybe—probably. Could she admit it? *Not.*

"What?" she asked out loud. "This isn't avoiding. See? Here you are, here I am."

Buffy looked doubtful. "So . . . we're cool?"

"Way," Willow said emphatically. *I'm not lying,* she told herself. *Just . . . stalling.* "That's why, with the party." She gestured at the jam-packed living room. " 'Cause we're all glad you're back."

Uncertainty shadowed Buffy's features, but she finally nodded. "Okay."

"Okay," Willow repeated. "Good." And she beat a quick exit back toward the band, knowing Buffy didn't feel any better but unable, yet, to do anything about it.

Downstairs, the band played and the people laughed, unconcerned, *unknowing,* about the evil slowly spreading itself via Joyce's Nigerian mask on her bedroom wall. She'd left all the lights on because of the party, and still the wicked red glow of its pulsating eyes outshone everything in the room.

* * *

The E.R. doctors and staff at Sunnydale Hospital had hoped for a quiet night, but no such luck. The guy on the table was a wreck, with third degree burns over most of his face, chest and arms. Still, the resident doctor diligently worked CPR, moving the man's chest up and down while a nurse forced air into his throat using a balloon. Nothing.

"Breathe—*breathe!*" His forehead slick with perspiration, the young doctor finally stopped. "What time is it?" he asked hoarsely.

"Seven forty-three," said an intern across the bed.

The resident grimaced. "Let's call it. It's been almost half an hour. These burns are too extensive—he's not coming back."

He turned away in defeat, but before he could take two steps the dead man on the table sat up, then lunged for him. The intern and the nurse both gasped and instinctively whirled back to the heart monitor still wired to the man's chest.

Flatline.

And screams filled the Emergency Room.

Buffy wandered through the party, wincing at some of the lame moves she was witnessing, trying to find someone, *any*one she knew.

"I think you'll be impressed," she heard a guy she thought was named Jonathan tell a cute girl as she passed. "It's the Cadillac of mopeds—"

The girl rolled her eyes and walked away and Buffy gave her a mental thumbs-up, amused at the way Jonathan sauntered off in the other direction as if he hadn't just received a brush-off. She found a niche where she could stand and nod in time to the music, at least *look* like she belonged here. That illusion was blown by the disturbing words of a couple of out-of-it guys she'd never seen in her life.

"Hey," drawled the smaller of the two to his buddy, "what's the deal with this party, anyway?"

"This party?" His friend looked completely out of it. "I heard it's for some chick who just got out of rehab."

Enough, Buffy thought. Like the girl dumping the Moped King a little while ago, she figured she'd rather be anywhere but here.

But escape wasn't easy. She angled out of the living room and ran straight into Cordelia and Xander when she turned the corner. Arms wrapped around each other, they obviously didn't need her company. Buffy did an about-face, but it was too late.

"Hey, Buff," Xander said. "What're you doing?"

"I was just . . . taking a break from all that wacky fun," she said, trying to back away.

Xander grinned and held on to his girlfriend. "Some party, huh? Guess a lot of people are glad you're back."

Buffy glanced toward the living room. "Seems like people I don't even know missed me. Did Giles say if he was going to be late?"

"He was library man last time I saw him. But he'll be here. He wants to celebrate your homecoming—we all do. I mean, it's great having the Buffster back." He smiled down at Cordelia. "Isn't it?"

"Totally," Cordelia agreed, looking surprised that Buffy was even there. She gave Xander a slinky smile. "Except, you were kind of turning me on with that whole 'boy slayer' look."

Xander's grin widened. "Was I now?"

"You bet," Cordy cooed. *"Nighthawk."* She giggled and nibbled on his ear.

"Well," Buffy said, since it was obvious Xander was

thinking about anything but Giles and the party. "I'll just be . . ."

She slipped away unnoticed.

In the kitchen, Joyce and Pat toasted each other with shots of frigid Peach Schnapps. They drank them down and took a deep breath, then beamed at each other over the empty glasses. "The kids have their fun, we have ours," Joyce said breathlessly.

There was a pause, then Pat gave Joyce a more serious look. "Now, how are you holding up, Joyce? Really?"

"Really?" Joyce considered this, then decided to be honest. "I don't know. While Buffy was gone . . . all I could think about was getting her home. I just knew that if I could put my arms around her and tell her how much I loved her, everything would be okay."

"But?"

Joyce looked at the table. "But things are never that simple, are they? I mean, she's here, she's right in front of me. So now I can *see* how unhappy she is. And I still don't know what to say—what to do—to make things right."

Pat nodded sympathetically.

Coming down the hallway, all a shocked Buffy heard were her mother's last two sentences:

"Having Buffy home," Joyce continued, "I thought it would make it all better. But in some ways, it's almost worse."

In the darkness outside, shadows gathered and moved, a small army of the undead.

And all aiming for the Summers house.

CHAPTER 4

Drat, thought Giles. *I really ought to get over to Buffy's party.*

But the research had taken longer than he expected—still no logical reason why this blasted cat had come back from the dead. He picked up the book on reanimation he'd looked at earlier and flipped through it. There must be something—

He froze.

"Oh, Lord," he whispered. He stared down at the illustration on the page, a rendering of a mask from Nigeria.

The same one hanging on Joyce Summers's bedroom wall.

Giles snatched up the telephone receiver and dialed Buffy's number, pacing as he waited for someone to answer.

"Party villa. Can I rock you?"

What was this? "Excuse me?" Giles said. "Hello?"

"What can I do you for, London-sounding guy?" asked the stranger on the other end. Music blared in the background, nearly drowning out the speaker's voice, Oz's concept of a hootenanny in full swing.

"I need to speak with Buffy," Giles said loudly, gripping the telephone cord. "Immediately. I have some information here that's extremely important—"

The sound of breaking glass followed by a cheer cut him off. "Yeah!" the voice crowed. "Fiesta foul! You gotta do a shot!"

"I need to speak to Buffy!" Giles yelled into the phone. *"Now!"*

"Buddy?" There was a pause and Giles realized the guy wasn't even listening to him. "That guy has to do a shot!"

"Buffy!" Giles yelled again.

There was another pause and the sounds of the party grew louder. Giles heard the speaker call out, could imagine him holding out the phone toward the room—as if anyone there could hear how desperate he was. "Hey, I need to talk to a Buddy. Is there a Buddy here?" After a moment, the voice came back in Giles's ear. "Sorry. He's not here. You got the wrong *casa*, Mr. Belvedere."

Dial tone.

"Hello? Hello?"

Exasperated, Giles slammed the phone down and grabbed for his coat. He'd just have to bring the bad news in person.

The lost look on Buffy's face had finally eaten far enough in to make her feel guilty, so Willow went to find her friend. When Buffy wasn't downstairs, Willow headed up—she had to admit that there were dozens of people here who were total strangers. With no one she knew to really talk to, maybe Buffy had retreated to the sanctuary of her own room.

Bingo, Willow thought. The door wasn't quite closed

and she saw Buffy moving around inside. She pushed it open, an apology on her lips, then froze.

Buffy was packing.

Everything she'd planned to say fled. "You're *leaving* again?" she demanded instead. "What, you just stopped by for your lint brush and now you're ready to go?"

Buffy didn't look up, just kept shoving things haphazardly into the duffel bag on her bed. "It's not like anyone'll mind."

"Oh, no, have a good time," Willow said. She couldn't keep the bitterness out of her voice. "And don't forget to *not write.*"

Buffy stopped. "Why are you attacking me? I'm trying—"

"Wow," Willow cut in. "And it looks so much like giving up!"

Buffy stuffed another wad of clothes into the bag. "I'm just trying to make things easier."

"For who?"

"You guys were doing just fine without me."

Willow stepped closer. "We were doing the best we could. It's not like we had a lot of *choice* in the matter."

"Look," Buffy said. Tears filled her eyes. "I'm sorry I had to leave, okay? You don't know what I was going through."

Willow stared at her. "Well, I'd like to."

"You wouldn't understand."

"Well, maybe I don't need to understand," she said, hurt. "Maybe I just need you to *talk* to me."

"How can I *talk* to you when you were avoiding me?" Buffy demanded angrily.

"This isn't easy, Buffy!" Willow inhaled. "I know you're going through stuff, but so am I."

"I know that you were worried about me, but—"

"No! I don't just mean *that*. I mean, my *life*. I have all sorts of . . . I'm dating. I'm having *serious* dating, with a werewolf! And I'm studying witchcraft and killing vampires, and I didn't have anyone to talk to about all this scary life stuff." Willow felt her eyes fill with tears as she faced Buffy. "And you were my *best friend.*"

Come on, you old car, Giles thought. *Come on!*

He pressed down harder on the accelerator, trying to coax another bit of speed out of the engine while his mind turned over the scene in Joyce's bedroom from earlier in the day. "Unbelievable," he muttered out loud. His voice went higher as he angrily mimicked Buffy's mother. "Do you like my mask? Isn't it pretty? It raises the dead!" He looked off to the side and scowled at the passing houses. "Americans."

Giles turned his gaze forward again, then opened his mouth in horror as he saw a man step directly in front of his car.

THUMP!

He saw the flash of a jacket as the person was knocked onto his hood, hit the windshield, then bounced off. Giles slammed on the brakes and leaped out of the car, rushing to where his victim lay facedown on the street.

"Are you all right?" he cried as he put a hand on the man's shoulder and rolled him over. "Are you hurt—"

The thing that opened its eyes and stared at him had been dead a long, *long* time. Giles jerked backward and from the corner of his eye he saw shadows lurching toward him—more reanimated corpses.

Before he could quite get to his feet, the dead man on the ground grabbed him.

Buffy's expression went shamefaced. "You have no idea how much I missed you, and everyone! I wanted to call every day."

"It doesn't matter, Buffy," Willow insisted. "It still doesn't make it okay that you didn't—" She broke off as Buffy's mother stepped into the room.

Joyce stared at the duffel bag in amazement. "What is this—is this some sort of a joke?"

"Mom," Buffy said. "Can you just . . . Willow and I are talking—"

But Joyce was not to be stopped. "No, I can't 'just'! Buffy, *what* is this?"

"She was running away again," Willow said accusingly.

Buffy took a step back "I—I wasn't. I mean, I'm not sure what—"

"Well, you'd better *get* sure and explain yourself right away!" Joyce cut in. "If you think you can just take off any time you feel like it—"

"Stop it!" Buffy cried. "Please! I don't know—I don't know what I'm doing!"

Before Willow realized what was coming, Buffy pushed past her mom and rushed out and down the stairs. But she wasn't getting away that easily—both Willow and Joyce were right on her heels. She saw her friend head for the front door, only to find it blocked by Xander and Cordelia, who were still lost in their own make-out zone. They broke apart and stared as they heard Joyce's indignant words.

"Don't you leave this house, young lady!" Buffy veered for the living room, now with all four of them after her. But the crowd was too thick for her to negotiate, and it was only a moment before Joyce had her by the arm. "You know what, that's *it!* You and I are going to have a talk!"

Willow saw Buffy's gaze cut to the people around her, who were backing away from the wrath of her mom and shaking their heads. "Mom, *please.*"

But Joyce's voice only got louder. "You know what? I

don't *care*," she announced, waving at the people in the room. "I don't care what your friends think of me, or you, for that matter. Because you put me through the wringer, Buffy. I mean it—and I've had Schnapps!"

The sounds of the party died away and Buffy stood there, center stage. Oz pushed his way through the kids and came to stand at Willow's side.

Joyce glared at her daughter. "Do you have *any* idea what it's been like?"

"Mom, this isn't the ti—"

"You can't imagine," Joyce told her. "Months of not knowing. Not knowing whether you were lying dead in a ditch somewhere or—I don't know. Living it up—"

"But you TOLD me!" Buffy's voice rose practically to a scream. *"You're* the one who said I should *go!* You said if I leave this house, don't come back! You found out who I really am and you couldn't deal. Don't you remember?"

Oh boy, Willow thought. She hadn't known about that part—but then, Buffy hadn't bothered to tell her, had she? Things were getting said here that maybe shouldn't be aired in public, but the anger was enough to make everyone forget that. She looked at Oz and saw him eyeing the party guests. Thankfully, a lot of them were edging out the door, not wanting to witness this family fight.

"Buffy, you didn't give me *time!*" Joyce cried. "You just dumped this *thing* on me and expected me to get it." She put her hands on her hips. "Well, guess what? Mom's not perfect! I handled it badly—but that doesn't give you the right to punish me by running away!"

"Punish you?" Buffy asked incredulously. "I didn't do this to punish you."

"Well, you did," Xander said, stepping forward. "You should have seen what you put her through."

"Great," Buffy said in disbelief. "Anybody else want

to weigh in here?" She spotted Jonathan a few feet away and gestured at him. "What about you, by the dip?"

Jonathan paused with a loaded chip almost to his mouth and shook his head, eyes wide. "No, I'm good."

"Maybe you don't want to hear it, Buffy," Xander told her, "but taking off like you did was incredibly selfish and stupid—"

"Okay," Buffy interrupted, her voice high. "I screwed up! I know this! But you have no idea. You have no idea what happened to me or what I was feeling!"

"Did you even try talking to anybody?" Xander demanded.

Willow felt a stab of pain as she saw Buffy swipe at tear-smudged eyes. "There was nothing that anyone could do. I just had to deal with this on my own."

"And you see how well that one worked out." Xander sent Buffy a disgusted look. "You can't just bury stuff, Buffy. It'll come right back up to get you."

Giles struggled with the putrid corpse holding him and finally broke free with a solid kick. He felt like a rugby player as he dodged through the zombies lining the street between him and his car, breathing a sigh of relief when he was again securely inside.

But the relief quickly turned to dismay when he realized he must have automatically yanked the keys from the ignition and pocketed them when he got out the first time. Now they gleamed in the glow of the streetlight—back in the center of the pavement.

"Oh, good show, Giles," he said darkly.

The undead were already crowding around the car and beating on it, trying to get at him. After a moment's thought, Giles slouched down in the seat and reached under the dashboard, hunting for the wires he knew would be accessible in this old model. The car rocked as the reanimated bodies hammered at it, and as he sorted through the wires and found the two he needed, he heard the passenger window cave in. Glass peppered him as the wires touched and finally sparked, and the engine grumbled to life. He shoved aside the flailing hand of a zombie, and stomped the accelerator.

"Just like riding a bloody bicycle," he said as he left the horde of walking stiffs behind. Despite everything, he was pleased with himself for remembering how to hot-wire the car.

"As if I could have even gone to *you*, Xander!" Buffy's face was dark. "You made your feelings about me and Angel perfectly clear."

"Look," Xander said sharply, "I'm sorry that your honey was a demon. But most girls don't hop a Greyhound over boy troubles."

"Time out, Xander." Willow and the others stared as Cordelia unexpectedly stepped forward in Buffy's defense. "Put yourself in Buffy's shoes for just a minute, okay?" She looked at the rest of them. "I'm Buffy, freak of nature, right? Naturally, I pick a freak for a boyfriend. Then he turns into Mister Killing Spree, which is pretty much my fault, and—"

"Cordy," Buffy interrupted. She looked completely horrified. "Get out of my shoes."

Cordelia threw up her hands. "I'm just trying to help, Buffy. If you haven't noticed, people aren't exactly lining up to give you props."

"Buffy," Willow began, "you never—"

"Willow, please," Buffy said pleadingly. "I can't take this from you, too—"

"Let her finish," Xander snapped. "You at least owe her that!"

Buffy glared at him. "God, Xander—do you think you could at least stick to annoying me on your own behalf?!"

"Fine," he said harshly, closing the distance between them. "You stop acting like an idiot, I'll stop annoying you."

Buffy's eyes narrowed and she stepped forward to meet him. Her fists squeezed together at her sides. "You want to talk acting like an idiot? *Nighthawk?*"

"Okay," Oz said suddenly, sliding smoothly between the two of them. "Gonna step in now, being referee guy."

"Let them go, Oz." Willow was so angry that her voice rose above everyone else's. "Talking about it isn't helping—we might as well try some violence."

Someone crashed through the living room window.

"I was being *sarcastic!*" Willow cried.

But no one heard her. The guy that had come through the window was being followed by someone else, then someone else again. He lurched through the living room, then stopped in front of some dude who along with everyone else was trying to escape to the door. Willow gaped in horror as without saying anything, the stranger grabbed the partyer's head and twisted it viciously. The party dude dropped like a limp rag.

The group went in different directions, but still, as always, instinctively worked together. As more breaking sounds came from the kitchen, Buffy leaned over and grabbed a fireplace poker. "Xander—the kitchen!" she yelled and tossed it.

Xander neatly snatched the poker from the air. "Got your back!"

He and Cordy headed down the hall and Willow turned to see Buffy pummeling the weird guy that had come through the window. Unnerved, Willow realized that no matter how many times Buffy beat him back, he just kept coming.

This time when the guy started to go for her again,

Joyce stepped up behind him and brought a heavy vase down on his skull. "Are these vampires?" she shouted at Buffy as he collapsed.

"I don't think so!"

At her side, Willow spied a piece of broken window sash, nice and sharp, and grabbed it. "Buffy, heads up!" she called and threw it.

Buffy's hand shot out. She caught and twirled the stake, then slammed it down into the center of her attacker's chest. He looked at her, then it, and fought to get up again.

"No," Buffy told her mother. "Not vampires."

Gee, Willow thought. *They walk, they* don't *talk, and if you stake 'em, they don't dust . . .*

Zombies.

CHAPTER 5

At the Summers household, the party continued.

By the front door, a terrified Pat was almost outside. Her luck didn't hold, though—only a couple of inches to go, but she didn't see the zombie step from the shadowed hallway behind her. She only felt its rotting hand cover her mouth as it dragged her back into the depths of the house.

In the kitchen, Xander and Cordelia did their best to beat back their own zombie. Xander picked up the bottle of Peach Schnapps and whacked it on the head; Cordy skewered it with a long barbeque fork. Nothing worked. "Man!" Xander exclaimed as he smacked it again. "This sucker wobbles but he won't fall down!"

In the living room, the others kept pounding on the creatures, to no avail. The chip and dips forgotten, Jonathan reached over and grabbed one of the band's guitars. "Not my guitar!" Devon barked at his side. "Use the bass!"

A few feet away, Buffy, Willow and Joyce still fought to control the same, unstoppable zombie. "He just keeps coming!" Willow cried.

"I know!" Buffy latched onto one of his flailing arms and pulled. "Try to get him back outside!"

Willow and Joyce jumped to help, and the three of them hauled the foul thing toward the front door. Oz was there with his hand on the knob.

"On three!" Joyce exclaimed. "One, two, *three!*"

Oz yanked open the door, then kicked at the zombies waiting outside before they could pile in. Willow and Joyce shoved their zombie out, using him like a bowling ball to take down the others. There was a harrowing moment as they fought to close the door against the hands trying to snake around its sides, then they turned the lock and leaned against it in relief.

"Help me barricade!" Buffy shouted. Devon, Jonathan and several others rushed to pile furniture and anything else they could find against the broken windows. "We need some help out here!"

In the kitchen, Xander sat hard on the zombie's back, forcing the thing's face to the floor as he finished trying it with telephone cord. "I got it," he told Cordelia. "Go help Buffy." She hurried to comply, joining the others as the last of the furniture was settled on top of their makeshift barrier.

"Great," Buffy said, drawing a much-needed breath. "Good job every—"

The center of the door crashed in as one of the creatures slammed its arm right through it.

The group scattered in all directions. Oz, Joyce and Cordy hightailed it for the stairs and Buffy grabbed Xander as he came out of the kitchen. "Upstairs!"

Oz and Cordelia pushed Joyce up in front of them, then found themselves cut off from the others as a zombie smashed through the weakened front door. They changed directions, forced back up toward the kitchen. "Oh, goody," Cordelia said curtly. "Back to the basement!"

But Jonathan, Devon and the others had made it there first, and the door shut firmly in their faces before they could stumble through. "Come on!" Cordelia yelled, pounding on it. "Let us in—it's Cordelia and Oz!"

"How do we know you're not a zombie pretending to be Cordelia?" demanded a terrified Jonathan from the other side of the door.

"Zombies don't talk!"

This time, it was Devon who answered. "But, how do we *know?* Maybe they do in real life—maybe only pretend zombies don't talk!"

Confused, Cordelia stopped with her fist raised. "Well . . . maybe they talk in real life but I think they would have deeper, sort of gravelly voices—"

Oz grabbed her wrist and pointed to the large zombie lumbering toward them. "Zombology can wait," he told her, and dragged her away.

Almost up the stairs, Joyce, Willow and Buffy stumbled over the unconscious Pat. They hauled her upright and dragged her into Joyce's bedroom. Buffy and Xander left Willow and Joyce to see to Pat while they built a new barricade, shoving the dresser and chair in front of the door.

Reluctantly, Willow leaned over and touched Pat's throat. No pulse. She looked at Joyce. "She's—" She didn't finish.

Grief flashed over Joyce's face. "Oh God—she's dead?"

But there was no time to think about it. Something splintered behind them and Willow and Joyce whirled to see a zombie had already managed to work its way partially through the door and the furniture piled in front of it. They hurried over to help, forced to leave Joyce's dead friend lying on the bed.

"What do we do if they get in?" Joyce asked in a panicked voice.

Xander pushed frantically against the widening gap in the door. "I kind of think we die!"

Fighting for their lives, no one noticed Joyce's Nigerian mask on the wall, its eye slits throbbing with deep scarlet.

On the bed, Pat's eyes slowly opened.

"Is that your foot?" Cordelia asked in the darkness.

"Oh," Oz said. "Sorry."

"I don't hear anything. Should we check?"

Oz considered this. "Go for it."

Cordelia found the knob and cautiously pushed open the door. They peered out—nothing. Carefully, both clutching ski poles, they inched out of the storage closet in which they'd been hiding. While there were muffled sounds elsewhere in the house, the downstairs seemed clear of any zombie action.

Upstairs then. They moved toward the front, rounding the first corner—

—and ran straight into Giles.

Both Cordy and Oz shouted in surprise and Cordelia raised the sharp end of her pole, ready to plunge it home.

"Cordelia!" Giles yelped. "It's *me!*"

She wasn't convinced. "How do we know it's really you and not zombie-Giles?" she demanded, brandishing the ski pole.

The librarian gave her an aggravated look. "Cordelia, do stop being tiresome!"

Cordy lowered her weapon. "It's him."

Oz tilted his head in the direction of the second floor. "I think the dead man's party has moved upstairs."

Giles nodded as they angled for the stairway. "That makes sense. It's the mask in Joyce's bedroom they're after."

"Mask?" Cordelia frowned. "They're here to exfoliate?"

Giles ignored her. "The mask holds the power of a zombie demon called Ovu Mobani—*evil eye*." They all stopped and looked toward the second floor, where they could see a knot of zombies fighting to get inside Joyce Summers's room. "I don't think we can get past them."

Oz lifted an eyebrow. "What happens if they get the mask?"

Giles's mouth was tight. "If one of them puts it on . . . he'll be the demon incarnate."

Cordelia glanced at him. "Worse than a zombie."

Giles looked at Cordelia, then again at the creatures gathered above them.

"Yes. Worse."

Despite their best efforts, one of the zombies had gotten through the door.

As Willow and the others fought with it, trying to figure out how to get it back out, Willow saw Joyce turn and look toward the bed. She followed the older woman's gaze to where Pat was pulling herself to a sitting position. Joyce hurried over to her.

"Oh, God—Pat," she said, nearly gasping with relief. "We thought you were—"

Before Joyce could finish, Pat shoved her aside and snatched at a weird-looking mask on the wall. Without hesitating, the woman brought the mask up and pressed it against her face. A demonic green light exploded from behind the thing, momentarily enveloping her.

When the group blinked away their surprise, they saw that the ugly mask, sharp teeth and all, had melded itself to Pat's skin.

Willow yipped as her hold on the zombie loosened. Now it cowered on the floor at their feet, trying to hide its face behind one decayed arm.

Joyce looked from it to Xander questioningly.

"Generally speaking?" he offered. "When scary things get scared? Not good."

The glow receded from Pat's face. *"I live,"* she intoned. Her voice was deep and echoing with power. *"You die!"*

Willow saw Buffy scowl and start toward the Pat-demon, then the Slayer was bathed in a nearly blinding white light that flashed from the eyes of the dead woman's mask. Horrified, Willow realized that whatever the light was, it had literally paralyzed Buffy. Before anyone could stop her, the Pat-demon advanced on the helpless teenager and brutally backhanded her.

Buffy went sprawling and Joyce's former friend turned on Willow.

"Willow, don't look!" cried Buffy from the floor, but it was too late. The light flashed again, and all Willow could do was stand there and send useless mental commands to her feet to run. Frozen in place, she felt the demon's hands on her head, ready to twist, and she had a memory-spark: Malcolm had done this same thing. She had escaped his attempt to kill her only to die now at the hands of a different demon.

"No!"

Head down, eyes averted, Buffy plowed full-speed into the Pat-demon.

Willow fell to one side. Buffy kept going in a full

body tackle that took both her and Pat right through the glass of the second story window.

Still trying to figure a way to get upstairs, Giles, Oz and Cordelia reversed course when they heard the explosion of glass and the crash of bodies rolling down the roof. There was a heavy *thud,* then sounds of fighting in the backyard. "Out back!" Giles commanded while upstairs in Joyce's bedroom, that struggle also resumed.

With Oz and Cordy close on his heels, Giles headed back down the stairs, but found them blocked by yet another zombie. The battle began, and Oz backed up, jockeying for a good kick to their zombie's head as Giles and Cordelia beat on it. "Oz!" Giles commanded between blows. "Tell Buffy—Mobani's power is in his eyes! She has to go for the eyes to defeat him!"

A split second decision and Oz changed his tactics, using his position as a springboard to vault over the other two and the creature on the stairs. A good thing, too—the zombie hit the space where Oz's rib cage had been hard enough to punch right through the wall.

The zombie in the room with them had, upon Pat's high-dive out the window, decided it should start fighting again. Willow, Xander and Joyce punched and kicked the thing, but it just wouldn't *stop.* Tossed against the outside wall, Willow sat, stunned, as Joyce reached beneath her bed and pulled out a sturdy baseball bat. She thought Buffy would have been proud to see her mother whaling on the creature in her bedroom with all her might.

And the two battles raged: one inside the room with her—

—and one outside with Buffy.

* * *

The creature that had become Pat found her footing first. She jumped on Buffy, knocking her to the ground and straddling her. Parroting the zombie who'd been so afraid of the Pat-demon, Buffy threw her arm over her eyes to avoid the paralyzing beam that kept pulsing out of the eyes of the mask. Caught off guard by her victim's tactic, the woman was thrown off by a right cross to the jaw. Buffy scrambled to her knees across the grass, searching for something at the edge of the flower bed—

Got it!

Buffy rose and spun—

—and looked straight into a flash of light from the demon's eyes.

She was stuck.

Darn, Buffy thought. All weaponed-up and no way to use it.

"Buffy!"

Startled, the Pat-demon whirled at the sound of Oz's cry and her paralyzing hold on Buffy broke. As the light from the creature's eyes immobilized Oz, Buffy hefted the gardening spade she'd plucked from the lawn. "Hey, Pat!"

The demon turned back, preparing to freeze her again. Averting her eyes, Buffy let instinct guide her hand as she drove the spade right through the eyes of the mask.

"Made you look."

Everything in the world seem to stop for a second, then an enormous bolt of white enveloped the Pat-demon. There was an unpleasant sizzling sound . . . then Pat vaporized, right in front of Buffy's eyes.

Willow saw the Pat-demon disappear, and when she glanced back to what was going on in the bedroom, she realized that Joyce was flailing with the bat at empty air. There was a crash downstairs and she heard Giles and

Cordelia shout in astonishment—whatever undead thing they'd been fighting had apparently also vanished, as had the rest of the creatures.

Another look out the window and there was her friend Buffy, dusting off her party dress with a satisfied look on her face. Best of all was her boyfriend Oz, standing cool and composed by the remains of the back door. She had no idea why Oz said it, but she heard his words clearly:

"Never mind."

Willow watched, smiling privately, as Joyce hurried to Buffy. "Honey, are you all right?"

Buffy's mouth quivered, just a little, and she reached out. "Mom . . ." Then they were hugging, as they should have all along, and Willow felt a bit of a sting in her own eyes as Buffy answered. "Yeah."

"So," Joyce finally said shakily. "Is this . . . a typical day at the office?"

"No." Buffy glanced at the wreckage in the living room. "This was nothing." She was only half-kidding.

Joyce looked appalled but she didn't have a chance to say anything as Xander stepped up to Buffy. "Nice moves."

She smiled slightly. "You, too."

The two slapped hands and Oz and Cordelia moved in to join with them, congratulating each other on another job well done. After a moment, Willow smiled and reached for Buffy, hugging her as tight as she could.

And, slightly back from the rest of them, Giles stood and watched as the Slayerettes found and accepted, once again, their Slayer.

He would not see them kept apart.

EPILOGUE

Giles knocked on Principal Snyder's door, then stepped inside his office without waiting for an invitation. He made sure to close the door behind him.

"Did we have an appointment?" Snyder asked in annoyance as he looked up from a pile of papers.

"I'd like to have a word with you," Giles said politely.

Snyder stood and walked around to the front of his desk. "If that word is 'Buffy,' then I have two words for you: 'Good,' and 'riddance.'" He picked up a folder and tucked a piece of paper into it. "Now, if you don't mind, I have an appointment with the Mayor."

Giles stood his ground. "You can't keep her out of this school."

Snyder gave him a nasty smile filled with little teeth. "I think you'll find I can."

"You had no grounds for expelling her."

Snyder's eyebrows shot up. "I have grounds. I have precedent. And a tingly kind of feeling."

Giles made an exaggerated show of courtesy. "Buffy Summers is a minor and entitled to a public education. Your personal dislike of the girl does not legally entitle you—"

Snyder dismissed him with a wave. "Why don't you take it up with the City Council?"

He started to step past Giles, but stopped at the librarian's next words. "I thought I'd start with the State Supreme Court. You're powerful in local circles, but I believe I can make life very difficult for you. Professionally speaking." Giles made sure his tone was pleasant. "And Buffy will be allowed back in."

Snyder hesitated, then his chin lifted in defiance. "Sorry. I'm not convinced."

As the man started to leave, Giles's hand came up and caught Principal Snyder across the collarbone, just below his neck. He shoved Snyder against the wall hard enough to hear the Principal's breath *whoosh* out of him. But when he spoke, Giles's voice never lost that agreeable tone. He was even smiling.

"Would you like me to convince you?"

Outside the sunshine was bright and the shopping district buzzed with noisy kids and parents. Inside the Espresso Pump, it felt cool and relaxing to Willow, a cozy place to reacquaint herself with her best friend. A perfect place to share a huge bowl of double chocolate ice cream with chocolate syrup and catch up on the missing chunks of both their lives.

"I mean," Willow said as she scraped up the last of the ice cream on her side of the dish, "I'm not like a full-fledged witch. That takes years. I just did a couple pagan blessings and a teeny glamour to hide a zit."

Buffy wrinkled her nose. "It doesn't scare you?"

"It has," Willow admitted. "I tried to communicate with the spirit world and I *so* wasn't ready for that. It's like being pulled apart inside. Plus I blew the power for our whole block—big scare."

Buffy looked half proud of her, and half wistful. "I wish I could have been there with you."

"Me, too." Willow smiled sheepishly. "I really freaked out."

"I'm sorry."

"It's okay," Willow said. "I understand you having to bail and I can forgive that. I have to make allowances for what you're going through and be a grown-up about it."

They sat there in silence for a moment, then a corner of Buffy's mouth turned up and she gave Willow the eye. "You're really enjoying this whole moral superiority thing, aren't you?"

Willow grinned. She couldn't help it. "It's like a drug."

"Fine," Buffy said, flouncing back. "Okay. I'm the bad. I can take my lumps . . . for a while."

"All right," Willow said, relenting. "I'll stop giving you a hard time." She looked at the table, then at her best friend again. "Runaway."

"Will!"

"I'm sorry." Of course she was, but she hadn't had Buffy to tease in *so* long . . . "Quitter."

Buffy glanced at her slyly. "Whiner."

"Bailer."

"Harpy."

Hmmm. That was pretty good. Willow considered her options for a moment: *Ah!* "Delinquent."

Buffy tilted her head, thinking. "Tramp."

Not even close, so Willow figured she might as well be just as ridiculous. "Bad seed."

Still, Willow had to laugh as Buffy managed to top everything they'd said so far with humor and, darn it, utter accuracy:

"Witch."

DAILY JOURNAL ENTRY:

It feels so good to have things back to normal.

Well, almost. I mean, I have every faith that Giles and Mrs. Summers will find a way to get Buffy back into Sunnydale High in no time. There's been like so much hardship and changes for all of us—I can't help but look forward to the school year with the belief that things *have* to get better. They do, don't they? Sure, this is the Hellmouth and there'll be monsters and demons . . . and probably a surprise or two. But with Buffy back, and all of us—me, Oz, Giles, Xander and even Cordelia—working together again, I feel like there's nothing that the Hellmouth can throw at us that we can't overcome. We are totally on top of it.

I've got Oz, and Xander and Cordelia have each other . . . as weird as that may seem. Sooner or later, Buffy will find someone new. And there's probably even a lady out there for Giles, don't you think?

If we can't find it ourselves, well... life has a funny way of working things out for us.

It just takes a little patience.

/Press Enter To Save File and Close Program/

ABOUT THE AUTHOR

Yvonne Navarro is a Chicago area novelist who has been writing for . . . well, a really long time. This is her eighth published novel and she's also published a whole bunch of short fiction and illustrations. She's just completed a psychological thriller called *That's Not My Name.* (Which is not about her—she really does know her own name.)

Her first published novel, *AfterAge,* was about the end of the world as orchestrated by vampires (imagine that), and was a finalist for the Bram Stoker Award. In her second novel, *deadrush,* she decided the concept of zombies really needed a new and interesting twist; *deadrush* was also nominated for the Bram Stoker Award. She's written the novelizations of both *Species* (for which actor Alfred Molina picked up the 1996 Audie Award for Best Solo Performance in an audiobook reading), and *Species II,* as well as *Aliens: Music of the Spears.* She also authored *The First Name Reverse Dictionary,* a reference book for writers.

Currently she plans to write a sequel to almost every solo novel she's ever written, and thinks they'll all be done by next Tuesday. Well . . . maybe not. But her readers are still requesting a sequel to *AfterAge,* as well as a third book to continue the unintentional miniseries of the award-winning *Final Impact* and its follow-up, *Red Shadows.*

ABOUT THE AUTHOR

The intensely curious can find everything from book excerpts to artwork to pictures of puppies and skydiving on Yvonne's web site, *Creaturette's Darke Palace*, at:

http://www.para-net.com/~ynavarro

Darke Palace also lets people know where Yvonne will be signing books and attending conventions, and where they can send books to be signed. There's even a message board on CNN.com's *Ask the Author* section—please visit!

Someday Yvonne plans to move to Arizona where she can sit and write in 100-degree heat amid the cacti, lizards and scorpions. She also plans to get another really big dog and name it something utterly diabolical.

Bullying.
Threats.
Bullets.

Locker searches? Metal detectors?

Fight back without fists.

fight for your rights:
take a stand against violence

Everyone's got his demons....

ANGEL™

If it takes an eternity, he will make amends.

Original stories based on the
TV show created by Joss Whedon
& David Greenwalt

Available from Pocket Pulse
Published by Pocket Books

2311

... A GIRL BORN
WITHOUT THE FEAR GENE

FEARLESS™

A NEW SERIES BY
FRANCINE PASCAL

A TITLE AVAILABLE EVERY MONTH

From Pocket Pulse
Published by Pocket Books